"Wh... we try to get you pre... as quickly as possible."

"And if I don't conceive?" Andrea challenged. Gabe's cold-blooded approach to something this sacred angered her.

"We'll deal with that when the time comes."

He was too shrewd an entrepreneur not to leave himself a loophole. *Oh, Gabe—you're so transparent.* He might just as well have pushed her off a cliff. A heart could only take so much....

What happens when you suddenly discover your happy twosome is about to be turned into a...*family*?

Do you panic?

Do you laugh?

Do you cry?

Or...do you get married?

The answer is all of the above—and plenty more!

Share the laughter and the tears as these unsuspecting couples are plunged into parenthood! Whether it's a baby on the way or the creation of a brand-new instant family, these men and women have no choice but to be

When parenthood takes you by surprise!

Look out for more books in this miniseries— coming soon in Harlequin Romance®!

THE BABY PROPOSAL
Rebecca Winters

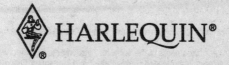

TORONTO • NEW YORK • LONDON
AMSTERDAM • PARIS • SYDNEY • HAMBURG
STOCKHOLM • ATHENS • TOKYO • MILAN • MADRID
PRAGUE • WARSAW • BUDAPEST • AUCKLAND

If you purchased this book without a cover you should be aware
that this book is stolen property. It was reported as "unsold and
destroyed" to the publisher, and neither the author nor the
publisher has received any payment for this "stripped book."

ISBN 0-373-03808-9

THE BABY PROPOSAL

First North American Publication 2004.

Copyright © 2004 by Rebecca Winters.

All rights reserved. Except for use in any review, the reproduction or
utilization of this work in whole or in part in any form by any electronic,
mechanical or other means, now known or hereafter invented, including
xerography, photocopying and recording, or in any information storage
or retrieval system, is forbidden without the written permission of the
publisher, Harlequin Enterprises Limited, 225 Duncan Mill Road,
Don Mills, Ontario, Canada M3B 3K9.

All characters in this book have no existence outside the imagination of
the author and have no relation whatsoever to anyone bearing the same
name or names. They are not even distantly inspired by any individual
known or unknown to the author, and all incidents are pure invention.

This edition published by arrangement with Harlequin Books S.A.

® and TM are trademarks of the publisher. Trademarks indicated with
® are registered in the United States Patent and Trademark Office, the
Canadian Trade Marks Office and in other countries.

www.eHarlequin.com

Printed in U.S.A.

CHAPTER ONE

"OY GEVEH!" Saul Karsh muttered before lighting the end of his cigar, the kind for which the Club Macanudo on the upper east side of Manhattan was famous. "You're *mishega!*"

"Actually, I've never been more sane," Gabe Corbin countered. He should have sold his company two years earlier. "Aside from Sam Poon who's already acting CEO, you're the first person I've told in case you want to buy me out. That gives you five days before I approach anyone else."

"What's the hurry? You're only thirty-six!"

"In my case that's already too old."

When Saul could see that Gabe wasn't about to enlighten him, he took a few more puffs on his cigar before he spoke. "If you're selling a billion-dollar company that's been operating in the black for years and is growing every day, then your reason must be personal." A hint of alarm entered his eyes. "You're not dying are you?"

"Of a disease? No." Gabe finished off the rest of his drink. "Send your people around tomorrow if you want to see the books. Phil Rosen's my chief accountant. He'll show you everything.

"Try to make a decision before Monday. By then I'll be gone and you'll be dealing with Sam."

Saul, the CEO of Karsh Technologies Inc., dealt in twenty-first century computers used for medical re-

5

search and the Space program. The acquisition of Corbin's Business PC's would give him another playing field altogether, one he'd wanted for quite a while if Gabe's source was right.

Saul was tough and aggressive, but Gabe knew of his reputation for fair business ethics. Of the five American entrepreneurs in the country who could buy Gabe out, he trusted Saul to be good to the employees and keep the company going in the right direction.

They stared at each other. Finally Saul muttered, "Stan Abrams and his team will be there at nine to take a look."

Those were the words Gabe had been waiting to hear. "Excellent." He put two twenty-dollar bills on the table and stood up. "It's nice seeing you again, Saul." He shook the older man's hand. "I hope we'll be doing business together."

"Gabe? I have a son who isn't much younger than you. If he were contemplating anything this enormous, I'd be worried. Are you absolutely positive you know what you're doing?"

The man's concern went a long way to prove to Gabe that Saul had been the right man to approach. "I know what I'm doing."

He left a bemused Saul sitting there puffing on his cigar. After exiting the bar, he climbed into the waiting limo.

"Benny? Take me back to the office."

"Yes, sir."

Now that Gabe had a probable buyer, there was work to be done. He rang Phil and Sam on his cell phone and asked them to come back to the office as soon as they'd finished dinner. In all probability they'd be working until midnight.

The process of divesting himself of the international business Gabe had built over the last fourteen years was a complicated one. But with Saul's people coming in the morning, Gabe could see light at the end of the tunnel, thank God.

As Gabe stood in the lobby waiting for an elevator to take him to the floor of his office, Bret Weyland, his North American sales manager, emerged from another one. For once Andrea Bauer wasn't with him. That was a surprise considering Bret had intimated he and Gabe's attractive chief software engineer, had been living together for the last three or four months.

Gabe could rarely find Andrea alone because Bret was always right there exhibiting a proprietorial interest in her that bordered on the possessive. It was a miracle Bret got any work done, or Andrea for that matter. But amazingly enough they did. Gabe had no room to complain.

He nodded to Bret. "Where's your other half tonight?"

"Cooking dinner at our apartment."

A vision of the two of them together behind closed doors doing anything and everything besides eating food disturbed him a great deal more than it should have. He wasn't walking away from his company any too soon.

"Lucky you." Gabe stepped on the elevator.

Bret flashed him a quick smile. "You're right about that," he said as the doors closed.

It was a good thing their conversation had been cut

short. Gabe had come within a hair's breadth of wiping that smug expression off the younger man's face.

At 9:30 a.m. Andrea hurried through the office to her boss's suite. His secretary looked up when she saw her. "Hi, Andrea. What can I do for you?"

"Is Mr. Corbin here?"

"Yes. He was already in when I arrived."

"Good. I need to talk to him right away."

"Just a minute and I'll see if he's free now."

"I'd appreciate that."

After the appointment with her gynecologist yesterday afternoon, Andrea knew what she had to do. There was no sense putting off the inevitable any longer.

"He says to go right in."

"Thanks, Karen."

She rushed into his private office. "Please forgive me for barging in like this when I know how full your schedule is."

His penetrating gaze swept over her. "Since when did you ever need to apologize for talking to me? You look upset, Andrea. Sit down and tell me what's wrong."

He talked to her in such a confiding tone, she did his bidding. "I saw my doctor yesterday and it looks like my endometriosis is coming back so I—"

"What did you say you have?"

"Endometriosis." Andrea disliked revealing something so personal about herself, but there was no way to avoid it now "It's a disease that seems to be the plague of the modern woman. Something to do with stress."

Her boss sat forward in his swivel chair eyeing her soberly. "Is this the reason you've had to take three personal leaves since coming to work for me?"

He'd been keeping track? How embarrassing! Yet he was being so kind, she found herself blurting the details.

"Yes. I've had six laparoscopies to be exact, the first one when I was in high school and the second in college. The third happened after I'd gone to work for Stover Electronics. That was before I interviewed for the position with your company."

She wouldn't have wished the emotional and physical pain of her disease on her worst enemy.

"I'm sorry, Andrea. I had no idea." His intelligent eyes shone with compassion. "What's the cure?"

"A hysterectomy. I've decided to have one as soon as possible. That's why I'm here. To arrange for the time off."

"You're only twenty-eight!" he exclaimed without addressing the main issue. "That's too young." He sounded as if he truly cared and Andrea found herself struggling not to break down in tears.

"Not in my condition. It happens to women during the childbearing years. I've been battling it since I was seventeen, but enough's enough. The doctor says I should plan on a six-week recovery period before coming back to work. I realize that's a long time to be gone, but I know Darrell won't let you down. He's a wizard."

Her boss grimaced. "There's nothing else to be done before you're robbed of the chance to ever carry a child?"

"Yes," she murmured reluctantly. "Get pregnant

right away before it grows back again worse than before, but that isn't a possibility.''

"Why not?" he demanded.

She had to admit it shocked her he kept firing questions of such a personal nature when all she was asking for was the time off to undergo the surgery.

Six months ago Andrea's degree in computer engineering, plus her work record at Stover's, had landed her a job at Corbin PC's. In the last four months she'd been serving as chief engineer of software which meant working part of every day with Gabe.

Even so, theirs had remained a professional relationship in the sense that he never pried into her personal life, and she knew next to nothing about his.

But she shouldn't have forgotten the driving force of his personality, or his native curiosity about life. Both traits had propelled him to heights even those in the world of high finance marveled over.

"This must be so difficult for you. Can you have children?" He prodded.

She shuddered.

Infertile. The dreaded word.

Being unable to conceive was another fear of hers. Maybe something was so wrong with her female reproductive system, her eggs weren't good. Unfortunately she would never have a chance to find out now.

"I have no idea," she answered at last. "I've never been married."

"But that hasn't precluded you from living with a man. I understand you and Bret have been liv—''

"The office gossip is wrong!" She cut him off.

What a fool she'd been to date Bret Weyland in the

first place. As head of Corbin's North American sales, he spent a lot of time working with Gabe, too. That was the only reason she'd gone out with him, to prove to herself Gabe didn't mean anything to her. Unfortunately everything had backfired and she'd hurt Bret in the process.

"That's odd," Gabe's deep voice came back. "Bret intimated just the opposite when we saw each other in the lobby last night."

Andrea let out an angry gasp. "Then he lied. I broke up with him over a month ago!"

"He's one of my top people. Why would he fabricate something like that?" her boss persisted.

She tossed her head back, causing her honey-blond hair to brush her shoulders. "Why does anyone when they're in pain? Look—if you must know, I've never slept with a man, let alone lived with one."

His pewter-gray eyes narrowed in disbelief. The lashes fringing them were as black as his curly hair. With such a proud nose, and jaws that needed shaving often, there had to be a generous portion of Southern European blood flowing through his veins.

"I don't know why that's such a surprise," she remarked when he didn't say anything. "There are lots of women who want a wedding ring on their finger first. However the joke's on me. I saved myself for marriage to my own detriment."

She heard the slight tremor in her voice and shot to her feet, mortified he might have detected it. Now was the time to say what needed to be said and get out of there before she broke down sobbing.

"My doctor has an opening in his surgery schedule next week. I'll work with Darrell today and tomorrow so he's prepared to take over. In six weeks you'll find he's the perfect person to replace me.''

Gabe's laserlike gaze might as well have pinned her to a wall. ''What's this all about, Andrea?''

It's about you.

''I once told you that my parents run a gift shop in Scarsdale. They've always wanted me to work in the family business. I told them I would when the time was right. Now that they're getting older and tire more easily, I can see that day has come.''

''Like hell it has,'' he bit out with uncharacteristic violence though he never raised his voice. ''You came in here asking for sick leave and ended up telling me you're going to quit. I'll fire Bret before I let that happen.''

''No—you mustn't do that!'' Her blue eyes implored him. ''The truth is, I turned him down when he asked me to move in with him. I'm not in love with him. He's only been trying to save face in front of you and everyone else.''

A strange look realigned the expression of Gabe's striking features, one she couldn't read. He sat back in the chair, eyeing her with disturbing scrutiny. ''I didn't realize.''

''You *can't* hold that against him.''

''I won't.''

''Thank you,'' she whispered in relief.

''You're welcome. I have to say your concern for him is admirable. Too bad more people don't have your decency.''

Her head lowered. ''Don't make me out to be a saint. I should have known better than to get involved with a colleague. It's a plan for disaster.''

Andrea was so in love with Gabe, she hadn't been aware of Bret's deepest feelings. Not until a lot of damage had been done. But no other man could compete with the one seated in front of her. His brilliant intellect and sheer male appeal made it impossible for her to see anyone else.

Though she'd been vehement in her denial, Bret had figured out she was in love with her boss and had accused her of it. Still, she had no idea his jealousy had driven him to tell Gabe something that wasn't true.

The whole situation had become untenable.

She took a calming breath and said, "Since I'll be recuperating at my parents' home, it will be the perfect time for me to resign. Darrell can consult with me over the phone during my recovery period. Your company won't feel a ripple."

"Have you considered your other option?"

His question tried her patience. "If you're talking in vitro fertilization from an unknown sperm donor, that holds no appeal whatsoever. I want the father around to help me raise our baby. A child deserves both parents."

"I couldn't agree more." He rubbed his thumb across his bottom lip. "If having the surgery right away is what you really want, I can't stop you of course."

The doctor had given her six months at the most, then she would *have* to undergo the surgery. But by then she would be in unbearable physical pain. The decision whether to do it sooner than later was an excruciating one. However if she had the operation now, she would be in better shape to go into the hospital and handle the impending ordeal.

Still, Andrea was devastated her boss didn't put up more of a fight to keep her with the company longer. "I—I'm glad you understand."

"Are you free of pain right now?"

"Yes."

"Then we'll fly to Paris this morning instead of next week as previously scheduled. I'd like Emile and his team to work with my expert software engineer before you're no longer available," he explained while she wrestled with her tortured thoughts.

Paris? Maybe that plan had been written in on Gabe's calendar, but this was the first Andrea had heard of it.

Since her promotion she'd been to Rio and Singapore on business with him, but never to Europe, the place she'd always wanted to go for a honeymoon. It was another pipe dream, just like the one where she gave birth to Gabe's child.

"We'll be staying through the weekend," he added. "How soon can you be ready to leave for the airport?"

Her last trip with him… She couldn't bear to think about it.

"I'll need a half hour to pack." Today was Thursday, which meant she would require four days worth of outfits. Knowing how Gabe operated, he would keep the team working through to Sunday afternoon when it was time to fly home.

"Benny will drive you to your apartment and wait for you. I'll see you at the plane. Don't forget your passport.'' He picked up the receiver and told his driver to meet her in front of the building.

Andrea left his office feeling like someone who'd been knocked unconscious and was starting to come to, yet everything remained fuzzy. She hurried past his private secretary Karen to her own office for her briefcase.

Corbin PC's corporate headquarters took up the twenty-ninth and thirtieth floors of the Saxbee building in downtown Manhattan. While she waited for an elevator to take her to the lobby, she said hi to a couple of the girls who'd just reported for work.

After a few minutes another elevator arrived going down. When the doors opened, Bret emerged in shirt-sleeves, carrying a file. The sales office was on the floor above.

''Andrea—''

''Hello, Bret.'' She entered the elevator, hoping he wouldn't join her. Thankfully he only stood there staring at her with wounded eyes until the doors closed.

That image of him stayed with her all the way out of the building to the waiting limo. It convinced her she was doing the right thing for herself and Bret by resigning. Gabe would never be able to replace him with anyone who could do a better job.

As for Andrea, her operation and recovery would take her out of Gabe's orbit for good. It was something that needed to happen for her own preservation, but his memory would haunt her forever.

Seven hours later a limo from Gabe's Parisian based company whisked them from De Gaulle airport to a suburb called Champigny. Soon Andrea found herself being escorted off the little rope and pully-operated raft on the swirling waters of the Marne River. Gabe explained they were staying on an island.

Somehow she'd assumed he would take her to a world-famous hotel like the Ritz, a favorite place for sheiks and millionaires. To her surprise and secret delight, he'd brought her to an isolated section of old-world charm.

The ambience, a combination of leafy trees and lush June foliage lining the riverbanks where there were a few fishermen in their berets, had transported her to another world so far removed from New York she could scarcely take it in.

The scene before her reminded her of a certain Renoir painting she loved. It depicted a group of local field hands in work clothes, gathered around a table enjoying a bottle of wine at the end of a long day. The concierge of the Vieux Pecheur Hotel could have been one of them.

He smiled when they entered the quaint little foyer. Andrea didn't think the two-story building contained more than half a dozen rooms for guests.

"Bonsoir, Madame, Monsieur."

"Bonsoir." Gabe set their suitcases on the floor. *"Je m'appelle Gabriel Corbin. Vous m'avez reservé deux chambres, n'est-ce pas?"*

"Oui oui. Remplissez l'affiche, s'il vous plaît."

Andrea blinked as Gabe started to register. She didn't know he could speak fluent French. He sounded like a native. If his parents were French, that would explain his dark, attractive features.

As soon as keys exchanged hands, Gabe picked up their cases and they climbed the tiny circular staircase to the next floor. He stopped at the first door on the left and opened it.

Andrea let out a soft gasp of delight.

Inside were two twin beds with green coverlets, a nineteenth-century armoire and dresser, plus a window that looked out on the quiet street. Checked gingham curtains in green and white adorned the frame. With a tiny fleur-de-lis print wallpaper on the walls and ceiling, the room was perfectly charming.

No phone. No TV.

This was the real France. A slice of life. That's what her college art teacher would have said about this incredible place.

"I adore it!"

"I thought you might," he drawled. "The bathroom's at the end of the hall. Everyone has to share." When she looked around at him, his lips were twitching. He was such a handsome man, her body quickened.

"My room's the next one on the right. I'll meet you in the foyer in ten minutes and we'll take a walk before dinner. I need to stretch my legs and imagine you do, too."

"Will Emile and the others be joining us later?"

"Not tonight." So saying, he left her to her own devices and shut the door.

That seemed odd, but maybe he was too tired to deal with employees and be social. As for Andrea, she was so excited to be in Paris, she was glad to put off work until tomorrow.

The first thing she did was run to the window and stick her head out to survey her kingdom above the foyer. The late afternoon light was fading into evening. As far as she could tell, of the few people who were passing by, none of them were tourists.

An older teen drew up on a bike with a few baguettes in the basket. He whistled before calling out something to her in his native tongue. Andrea couldn't help smiling before she turned from the window and headed for the bathroom where she could freshen up.

The old-fashioned lock didn't look like it could keep anyone out, but she honestly didn't care. This was the kind of adventure you dreamed about, but rarely experienced.

She examined her cream linen skirt which was somewhat wrinkled after their flight. Luckily the mango-colored cotton top never creased.

After rummaging in her purse, she combed her hair and applied some coral lipstick. Thank goodness she'd chosen to wear her comfortable Italian leather sandals. She'd be able to walk around without problem.

Andrea had just reached the foyer when a male voice in a heavy French accent said, "I was hoping the beautiful American woman would come down soon."

The guy she'd seen moments ago had put his bike behind the front desk. Up close he looked like he might be twenty, twenty-one. His Gallic features resembled the male concierge who'd checked them in earlier.

There was no sign of Gabe.

"I'll have to tell my girlfriends to stay here when they come to Paris if they want some fun," she teased.

He grinned. "You're not sleeping in the same room with your friend. That means you might go out with me tonight? I could show you a very good time. My name is Pierre.''

She chuckled. ''That's a tempting offer, Pierre, but I'm here on business.''

His hooded eyes dwelt on her face. ''You work for him, or does he work for you?''

Pierre would be shocked if he knew who Gabe was. ''He's my boss.''

''What is wrong with him?''

''Excuse me?''

''He brings you to Paris and doesn't share your bed? That I cannot understand.''

''No one asked you to,'' a low, chilling voice broke in on them. Gabe had descended the staircase without her being aware of it. He'd changed into a black silk shirt and gray trousers.

She'd never seen him dressed in anything but a suit. The transformation brought out a potent masculinity that took her breath. But his chiseled features revealed an aggression directed at the younger man.

''He didn't mean any harm,'' Andrea whispered. ''Let's go.''

She could feel the rigidity of his body before he put his hand on the back of her waist and ushered her out of the hotel. The heat of his touch seemed to burn through her top.

When they'd walked past the adjoining patisserie he said, ''I'm sorry you were subjected to that. I won't leave you alone again.''

Andrea turned to him. ''I've met boys like him before.''

Gabe's jaw hardened. ''He's no boy, Andrea, and he's on the make for any willing female.''

"So are a lot of guys his age."

His eyes studied her features. "I suppose after the way you defended Bret, I shouldn't be surprised."

"No, you shouldn't." She smiled as she said it. "I'm sure he feeds the same line to all women young or old who stay at the hotel. An extenuation of his job. Keep the customers happy."

One dark eyebrow quirked. "Did it make you happy?"

"Well—yes, in a way. It's a fun memory to take home with me."

After a long silence he said, "I'll have to remember that."

His dark mood had passed.

For half an hour they made desultory conversation while they walked beneath the cathedral of trees. The soft, warm summer air played havoc with her senses and seemed to be affecting him, too. Andrea took care not to brush against him. The slightest contact of his leg or arm sent a live current of electricity through her body.

She should have been relieved when Gabe broke the spell by stopping to speak to one of the fishermen around a bend in the river. The older man didn't seem to be having any luck, but whatever her boss said brought a light to his eye.

From his tackle basket he drew out another type of lure and put it on the end of his line. Then he began casting. Before long he had a fight on his hands. After he'd reeled in a nice-size fish, he grinned and patted Gabe on the shoulder.

"What kind is it?"

"Carp."

"I've never tasted it."

"Smoked carp is out of this world."

"You're full of surprises," Andrea said as they started to circle back. "Were you born here in France to know what kind of bait would catch it?"

He darted her a curious glance. "No, I'm a native of St. Pierre et Miquelon."

She frowned. "Is that in Belgium or Switzerland?"

"Neither. It's a French territorial collectivity off the coast of Newfoundland."

The mention of the Canadian province rang a bell.

"That's right!" She stopped walking. "I remember my junior high geography teacher telling us about some islands being the only French possessions remaining in North America. A big fishing industry. As I recall, she said Al Capone used to hide out there during prohibition."

One corner of his mouth lifted. "You have a keen memory and know more about it than ninety-nine percent of the world. I'm impressed."

"I'm flabbergasted. I've never met anyone who came from there. Your English is so perfect, I had no idea."

"My mother's an American. I hold dual citizenship."

"Is your family still there?" She wanted to know anything and everything about him.

A shadow entered his eyes, but it was fleeting. "Yes."

"So how come you left?"

"I had a yen to explore the world."

"And look what happened!" she blurted with a

smile. ''But your fishing roots still have a hold on you.''

He nodded. ''I serve on the French Fisheries Board. As a result, I'm aware of problems on the Marne after last year's champagne harvest.''

Andrea was totally intrigued. ''What happened?''

They began walking again.

''The heavy September rains washed pomace and excess grapes into the river. There's been a massive cleanup effort to get rid of the dead fish lining the banks. I'm glad to see the old man was able to catch something.''

So his chat with the fisherman was no idle conversation.

''What's your specific job on this board?'' By now she had so many questions to ask, she couldn't fire them off fast enough.

''To help settle maritime boundary disputes between France and Canada's fishing territories.''

Good heavens. That would be a full-time job in and of itself. Only a man of his extraordinary abilities could take that on and run a billion-dollar corporation in the process.

''Is your island's fishing industry in trouble?''

He stared hard at her. ''If you really want to know, I'll answer your questions while we eat dinner.''

As if he did it every day, he slid his arm around her shoulders and guided her toward an adorable sidewalk café a few doors up from the hotel. It was the kind of place just for lovers, with bistro chairs and small round tables covered in red and white checked cloths.

A few couples were dancing to an old French love

song played by a roving accordionist. As soon as Gabe
seated her, a waiter appeared with two glasses of white
wine. Another waiter brought some freshly baked
bread still warm from the oven.

"They only serve one entrée here so there's no
menu," Gabe explained when they were alone. "You
haven't lived until you've tasted their fried moules."

Andrea decided she hadn't lived until she'd entered
this land of enchantment with Gabe. She feared she
was in the middle of a fantastic dream and was going
to wake up at any second.

CHAPTER TWO

WHILE they sipped their wine and ate the mouthwatering bread, Andrea cast Gabe furtive glances.

The flicker of candlelight revealed the amazing color of his eyes. She'd always thought them a solid gray, but tonight the outer rim of his irises gleamed silver. With his head of swirling black hair and a five-o'clock shadow covering the lower half of his face, he was the most sensational looking man she'd ever seen.

"Bon appetit," the waiter said after placing side dishes of French fries and a hot platter heaped with mussels in front of them.

Gabe's eyes met hers. "They've been cooked in a sauce of white wine, garlic and cream. Try one and you'll understand."

The fragrance tickled her nose. After she took her first bite, she couldn't stop.

"My grandmother used to cook moules this way. My brothers and I would have contests to see who could eat the most."

Andrea chuckled, wishing she could have been witness to such a sight. "I can see why. I've never tasted anything so delicious."

The confidences coming bit by bit were starting to fill in the gaps that explained the man behind the corporate mask. When Andrea was finally full she put down her fork. "So, when did your grandmother pass away?"

He finished off his wine. "Two years ago."

"I'm sorry." Maybe he didn't like all her questions, but she was hungry for answers only he could give. "Do you have a big family?"

"I'm the second of four brothers, two of whom are twins."

Twins—

"How lucky for you. I'm an only child."

"They're all married. At last count I have seven nieces and nephews. There's my father Giles, of course; my grandfather Jacques, two aunts with husbands, children and grandchildren."

No mention of his mom...

"Everyone lives in the same neighborhood in St. Pierre and derives their livelihood from the sea. The first Corbin we know of came from Brittany and was fishing those waters when Jacques Cartier stopped there on his return to France in the mid-fifteen hundreds."

Fascinating. "What about your mother's side of the family?"

"I have a lot of relatives in Chicago."

"How on earth did your parents meet?"

"Mother was coming home from a trip to Europe when her plane had to be diverted to Halifax. She and my father were both stranded at the airport for the better part of a week due to a ferocious Atlantic storm. One thing led to another and he took her home to meet the family. They married, had children. She divorced my father when I was eighteen."

The unexpected revelation pierced her heart. His

parents' breakup would have done terrible things to his emotions, yet he'd channeled that hurt and anger to build an empire. If he hadn't gone down that path, Corbin PC's might not have been, Andrea might not have ever met him. The thought made her ill.

"We survived, Andrea. Though my mother has never discussed the divorce, she and I have remained close. We see each other often. She works for a travel agency and flies to St. Pierre to visit my brothers every month."

It was just as well one of the waiters chose that moment to clear their dishes. Andrea wanted to get to know Gabe better. She could see the pain in Gabe's eyes as he talked about his past.

Another waiter followed with two plates of melon chunks. The dessert looked simple enough until she tasted it. "Oh—I don't believe anything could be this divine."

Gabe's eyes were smiling. "It's the champagne glaze."

Between his nearness and the effect of the wine after all the delicious food they'd eaten, she was dangerously close to floating.

"You were going to tell me about the problems your island is facing."

"Later," he murmured. "Right now I want to dance with you."

Her heartbeat accelerated to a galloping pitch as he grasped her hand and drew her into his arms.

She'd heard "La Vie en Rose" many times in her life, but she'd never danced to the live music of an authentic French accordion player before. Gabe's hard muscled body seemed to meld with hers. She buried her face in his shoulder.

"Are you having a good time, Andrea?"

The question made her a little crazy. She was in heaven, but she couldn't tell him that. "Thanks to you I'm having an unforgettable experience."

"Then look at me."

She clung to him even tighter. "I'm afraid to."

"Why?"

"Because I smell of garlic."

His body began to shake with silent laughter. "We both do, so there's no problem."

She finally raised her head, but the slight motion caused her to feel dizzy. "I—I wish I had some gum."

"I'd rather taste the champagne on your lips." In the next breath his tempting male mouth closed over hers in a warm kiss that seemed so natural, she opened hers involuntarily.

While they moved around the dance floor, their kiss slowly deepened and became a part of the total magic of the night. One song turned into another, one kiss grew into another. Andrea had no idea how long they communed in that halcyon state.

Gabe had begun kissing her cheeks and neck and hair, and she was making little moaning sounds while she let him. She'd forgotten they had an audience until they'd stopped dancing.

A wave of heat engulfed her at her loss of control. Breaking away from him, she walked past other diners to their table on unsteady legs to get her purse. She hadn't drunk that much wine and couldn't blame the alcohol for her reckless behavior. It was Gabe who'd turned her into some kind of sybarite.

Without waiting for him, she left the café and headed for the hotel. Pierre's father stood behind the front desk, thank goodness. He nodded to her. She flashed him a smile and kept walking.

Gabe caught up to her on the staircase. When she sensed him behind her, she ran up the last few steps.

"What's the hurry?" By this time they were both standing outside her door. She was breathless.

"I got a little carried away on the dance floor and figure it's past my bedtime."

His low chuckle resonated to her bones. "I should have brought you to Paris long before now. It's wonderful watching someone else react to it for the first time."

"You made it wonderful by bringing me here, Gabe. I'll never forget it." Her voice was trembling again. "Good night." She put her key into the lock and opened the door.

"Andrea?"

Her heart thudded in her chest. "Yes?"

"Thank you for giving me a memory. I'll come by for you at eight-thirty in the morning. We'll raid that pastry shop next door before we do anything else. Sleep well," he whispered before walking off.

There was no possibility of that now. He'd made the night too magical for her.

Grabbing her toiletries, she hurried down the hall to get ready for bed. But she knew she would stay awake most of the night reliving every thrilling moment with him.

A creature of habit, Andrea woke up at six-thirty though her body craved more sleep. Gabe wouldn't come knocking for another two hours.

Unwilling to lie there in fresh anticipation of seeing him without being able to do anything about it, she dressed for work in a matching cotton blouse and skirt in a khaki color. When she'd done her hair and makeup, she packed her bag and carried it downstairs.

This time she encountered a woman at the front desk who was probably Pierre's mother. The older woman greeted her.

"*Bonjour,*" Andrea responded in kind.

"Monsieur Corbin is next door eating breakfast." Gabe was already up? "You are welcome to leave your suitcase with me while you join him."

"Thank you."

After the woman came around to take it from her, Andrea walked outside to an overcast sky filled with the most amazing cloud formations. She discovered tables and chairs set up in front of the patisserie. Gabe sat at one of them dunking a croissant in his coffee before eating it while he read the *Figaro*.

In thigh molding jeans, a burgundy T-shirt and sneakers, he gave off a sexual male aura that made her heart leap. But it was hardly the attire she expected him to wear to work.

Since her talk with him yesterday morning, nothing had gone the way she'd thought. There was no possibility of second-guessing him. It was one of the many aspects about him that increased his desirability.

As she approached, he looked up from the newspaper. His glance was swift but thorough, otherwise she wouldn't be feeling this sudden weakness. He got to his feet in one lithe movement and helped her to sit down.

"I can never sleep in, either," he murmured before

removing his hand from her arm. Her skin continued to feel his imprint even after he'd taken his place once more.

"It's just as well. I'm sure Emile wants to get started as soon as possible. If we hurry and settle down to business, he won't have to keep his team working through the whole weekend."

Gabe poured her a cup of hot coffee from the carafe without commenting. Apparently he'd been expecting her at some point. Unlike him, she was as predictable as the sun rising every morning. After last night she feared her attraction to him was transparent.

The woman who ran the shop brought out a plate of golden croissants.

"Try one," he said. "They're filled with spinach and feta cheese."

She trusted him to know what was good and took a bite. He was right. It was a gourmet's delight. But she had a fluttery sensation in the pit of her stomach that robbed her of an appetite. She reached for the coffee instead.

Gabe appeared so calm, it convinced her he'd forgotten what had gone on between them last night. "It feels like it might rain."

"But it won't," he said, eyeing her over the brim of his cup.

"How soon is Emile expecting us?"

"He isn't."

She almost choked on her coffee. "I don't understand."

"Then I'll clarify things for you." He put down his cup and leaned forward, staring at her through veiled eyes. "I brought you to Paris for one reason only."

She didn't know Gabe like this. "If you're talking about seducing me, you had your chance last night—" she joked because she didn't have the slightest clue what was going on in his mind, let alone where this conversation was headed.

To her shock he didn't laugh or even smile.

"You're way off base, Ms. Bauer." He hadn't called her by her last name since the first day she'd interviewed with him.

Heat rose in her cheeks. "You think I don't know that?" Talk about twisting the knife till blood gushed.

"I've never proposed marriage to a woman before, and thought this the ideal place."

Marriage—

The cup slipped from her hands, spilling some of the coffee on her blouse.

"S-sorry I'm so clumsy," she stammered as she dabbed at the stain with a napkin. "I must have misunderstood what you just said."

"You mean about my asking you to be my wife?" His hand covered hers, stilling it.

"You're joking of course—"

"I never joke."

She knew that.

His was a serious nature, even brooding. The man worked harder than anyone she knew, and expected the same from the people around him. She doubted he had a frivolous bone in that tall, powerful body she found undeniably appealing.

Sometimes she glimpsed a mystifying streak of melancholy that tore at her heartstrings. After their conversation last night, she thought she understood part of the reason for it.

"You don't marry someone when you're not in love," Andrea whispered, struggling to find her voice.

"We like each other." He inserted the irrefutable fact in the same way he made a polarizing comment at a board meeting, inevitably silencing everyone. "All you have to do is remember last night to know it's true."

Last night...

She hadn't been able to think about anything else. It had haunted her dreams and made her so restless she'd wanted to steal to his room and beg him to make love to her.

"Who's to say 'like' isn't preferable to love that can twist and torture the soul." Gabe's rhetorical question was proof his parents' divorce had crippled him emotionally, just as she'd thought.

"Admit we have an excellent working relationship, Andrea. We know each other better than anyone else. I don't recall us ever having a serious disagreement. There's no doubt we're sexually compatible." The thumb caressing her palm was sending little darts of awareness through her system.

"You're crazy!" As if she'd just been stung, she pulled her hand away. Beyond pain, she said, "I've worked with you long enough to know Gabe Corbin never does anything without it being part of a grand design."

He sat back. "That's true."

She eyed him frankly. "What's the real reason you've picked on me to enter into a loveless marriage?"

After subjecting her to an intimate appraisal he said, "I'm not about to allow you to throw away your chance to give birth to your own child if I can help it. We'll make it our top priority.''

They were back to a discussion of her female problem. "*You* want to give *me* a baby—'' she mocked.

"Barring unforeseen circumstances, yes, I'd like to give you a child. I want us to marry so that you can have our baby.''

She sprang to her feet and put her fists on the edge of the table. "What's going on?'' she demanded. "And don't tell me you want to do this for me out of the kindness of your heart! What's in it for you?'' By now her curvaceous five-foot-five body was leaning toward him.

Lines darkened his features making him look all of his thirty-six years. "A way to atone for my sins,'' he answered in a gravelly voice.

It never failed that when Andrea asked him a pointed question, he always came back with an unexpected answer that confounded her. This one reached a spot deep in her soul and she quietly sat down. "What sins?''

"When I left St. Pierre for college, Jeanne-Marie, one of the girls from the island, came to my apartment in New York.''

Andrea knew there had to be a Jeanne-Marie-whatever-her-last name-was somewhere in his past.

"She claimed she hadn't wanted me to leave home and was hoping I would marry her.''

If anyone understood what it was like to love Gabe, Andrea did. The heartbroken girl would have been in agony to watch him walk out of her life.

"That was a ludicrous announcement on her part

since Jeanne-Marie and I had no past together. She knew there could never be a future.

"The truth is, we slept together one time. I'm not proud of the fact that I had a one-night stand, but I did and marriage was the last thing on my mind where she or any woman was concerned.

"I told her to go back to St. Pierre. Later on I received a call from my father that she was going to marry my brother Yves."

The picture was getting clearer. When Jeanne-Marie couldn't have Gabe, she chose the next best thing.

"It pained me to realize I'd been with a woman my brother loved enough to marry. He deserved to know the truth about Jeanne-Marie and me before things went any further, so I made plans to fly back to the island to talk to him. But my father told me something that changed my life."

Andrea had a premonition where this was leading. Her eyes closed tightly and she sat back down in her chair.

"He said she'd just suffered a miscarriage. Though everyone thought it was Yves's baby, he knew differently, meaning *I* was the father. My father suggested that for Yves's happiness, it might be wise if I never came back."

"Gabe—" Gut wrenching pain tore through her. "Do you mean to tell me you've never been home since?"

Emotion darkened his eyes until she couldn't see any silver. "I flew in the day my grandmother was buried, but waited till night to visit her grave. Grandpère was there alone. We talked until first light, then I left the island."

She shook her head, aghast to think of his being estranged from his family all these years. "Why didn't Jeanne-Marie tell you she was pregnant when she came to see you?" her voice trembled.

"The night we were together I took precautions which let her know I didn't want there to be any consequences. She was probably afraid to tell me she'd gotten pregnant."

"But it was *your* baby!" Andrea said emotionally. "You had a right to know."

He folded his powerful arms. "I agree. However at eighteen who's thinking clearly?"

"*You* were, otherwise you wouldn't have left home to follow your dreams."

"I got out of there because I couldn't stand to see the pain in my father's eyes after he and mother divorced."

Andrea believed him, but whether he realized it at the time or not, she knew other forces had been at work prompting him to fulfill his destiny.

"I'm so sorry, Gabe." She wished there were a better word besides sorry to convey her feelings. "I— I still don't understand how marrying me would help you atone for your sins."

He sucked in his breath, "You haven't lived with my guilt. Jeanne-Marie needed me and I rejected her."

"You wouldn't have, *if* she'd been truthful with you!"

A wintry smile came and went. "Thank you for defending me, but it doesn't relieve me of blame. I slept with her when I didn't love her."

"She sought you out because she was willing, Gabe. That makes her share equally in the blame."

"Maybe," he conceded, "but if I'd married her, she might not have had the miscarriage."

Her heart ached for him. "You're beating yourself up for something you were helpless to rectify without knowing all the facts."

He shook his dark head. "None of that matters now. Our baby didn't survive, and there's been no way for me to make restitution. When you came to me yesterday morning, I sensed your desperation and realized there *was* something I could do for you before it's too late."

She averted her eyes.

"Knowing what was at stake, I admired your honesty in not using Bret who was obviously ready and willing to make you his wife, something I wasn't prepared to do for Jeanne-Marie..." His voice trailed. "I believe we could make a marriage work, Andrea. We have no secrets, only the hope of getting you pregnant."

Andrea looked up at him again. His eyes shone with an intensity she'd never seen before. If she didn't miss her guess, he wanted a baby to replace the one his father had told him he'd lost.

Her stomach clenched because she was holding back a lie of her own by not revealing that she was in love with him. But how could she open up to him? He wasn't asking for her love any more than he'd asked for Jeanne-Marie's...

"I'm far from perfect, Gabe."

He shrugged his broad shoulders, drawing her attention to the movement of rock-hard muscles beneath his T-shirt. "Our relationship would be built on honesty, not perfection.

"What I'm proposing is that we get married immediately and try to get you pregnant as quickly as possible."

"And if I don't conceive?" she challenged. His cold-blooded approach to something as sacred as marriage angered her.

"We'll deal with that when the time comes."

"You mean divorce."

After a pause, "Only if it's what we both want."

He was too shrewd an entrepreneur not to leave himself a loophole. *Oh Gabe—you're so transparent.* He might just as well have pushed her off a cliff. A heart could only take so much.

"There *is* one condition. For fathering our baby and bestowing my worldly goods on the two of you for the rest of our lives, you would have to agree to it."

She knew there had to be a condition! In fact she'd been waiting for the other shoe to fall.

If she were to marry him and they divorced, naturally he wouldn't be ecstatic about parting with half of those worldly goods which included a billion dollars or more.

Andrea couldn't comprehend that amount of money any more than she could comprehend the damage done to him by his parents and Jeanne-Marie.

"Beyond a healthy respect for the way you've made your money by the sweat of your brow, I would never want to have your wealth. The responsibility would be…frightening."

"I'm well aware of that," came the surprising rejoinder. "When you're in my position of having lived hand-to-mouth before making a fortune, you acquire a sixth sense about people. I've learned to choose my associates carefully.''

He subjected her to an intense regard. ''If you had been a gold-digger, you would never have made it through our first interview.''

A shiver ran down her spine. She imagined many women, ambitious and otherwise, had tried without success to pierce his impregnable armor. How could they know a scarred soul lived inside such a successful man?

''Don't you want to know what my condition is?''

She shivered.

When Bret had started dating her, he'd told her there was a ruthless side to Gabe's nature. Otherwise he wouldn't have become a billionaire by the time he was thirty-six.

Andrea had laughed off the comment because she'd never witnessed that trait in Gabe. Though he'd always been somewhat aloof, everyone in the company admired him. He treated his employees fairly and cared about them. The man commanded the highest respect from people worldwide.

But she'd seen multiple sides of him since coming to Paris and felt no urge to laugh. In fact she was in a state of absolute panic because she could feel herself caving even though she knew he wasn't capable of loving her or any woman.

''Gabe—''

''I'm going home to St. Pierre.''

She blinked. ''You mean you want to take me with you for a visit?''

''No. It'll be for good. Yves and Jeanne-Marie now

have two teenage children, I'm no longer a threat to their marriage. I miss the sea…and home.''

''But your company—''

''I'm selling it and funneling the money into a perpetual fund for the welfare of the island which has been in economic crisis for years.''

He was giving away his billion dollars? Just like that? ''When did you make this decision?''

''A long time ago. Since my family wouldn't let me help them financially, I had to find another way to do it. The point is, I always intended to go back, and have stayed in touch with my grandfather.

''However since my grandmother's death, he has been depressed. To make matters worse, his friend from childhood, Gorka Zubeldia, who lived next door passed away recently. His widow Karmele is planning to move to the Pyrenees any day now to join their son.''

''So you weren't the only son to leave the island.''

He flashed her another penetrating glance. ''No. When Grand-père told me that news, I had my realtor buy the Zubeldia's house for me without Grand-père's knowledge. It has possibilities.''

''Possibilities? In other words, it will need a lot of work.''

His lips twitched. The sight was so rare, it was hard not to stare. ''Until it's vacant, we'll stay with Grand-père. I'm hoping my return will raise his spirits and help him to enjoy the years he has left. The Corbins are known for their longevity. He's only eighty-one.''

She studied Gabe for a long moment. He seemed to have planned everything down to the last detail. It was all going so fast. "He has no idea you're coming, does he."

"No. But the day I left St. Pierre, my grandparents told me their door would always be open. That has never changed over the years. The house holds many choice memories for me.

"Nevertheless it's an isolated world, Andrea, and in some ways very harsh. Naturally I'm going to keep enough money in trust for you and our child so that if anything happened to me, you would be taken care of.

"But I'm speaking of the total picture, of the fog and the interminable ice and cold of winter. Few outsiders can make it in such an insular society of people who tend to stick to their own and draw their livelihood from the sea.

"But it's my home. If I had a child, that's where I would want to raise it. No son or daughter of mine is going to grow up any differently than I did."

What an extraordinary man he was.

"Except for my father and grandfather, the family doesn't know the real reason I never came home again. They believe I'm a traitor who left the island because hard times hit economically.

"Because of their resentment of me abandoning the life I was born to—an action they consider to be a sin—the family will crucify you by their unwillingness to get to know you. They might never accept you. I'm telling you all this so there won't be any surprises in case you decide to marry me.

"I'd like your answer by tonight," he murmured. "In the meantime we'll tour Paris to your heart's content."

She doubted any woman had ever received such a bizarre marriage proposal.

What a choice— Never see him again, or live with him under almost untenable, if not impossible, circumstances. *You're damned whether you accept or not, Andrea.*

"You've given me so much to think about, I'm afraid any sightseeing would be wasted on me." She pushed herself away from the table and stood up. "If you don't mind, I'd like to fly back to New York today."

"So be it. I'll send for a limo and alert my pilot you're on your way to the airport now."

She bit her lip. "You're not coming, too?"

"No. I have business at the fisheries board and will fly home later on a company plane." He cocked his head. "Don't take too long making up your mind. It would be a crime to delay, if you only have five months to conceive.

"Though I only slept with Jeanne-Marie one time, there's no guarantee I could make *you* pregnant that fast, but I'm prepared to try."

Such brutal honesty was hard to take. Andrea would have welcomed even one tiny white lie such as, "I've had my eye on you for a long time, but knew you were involved with Bret."

He poured himself another cup of coffee. "When I'm back in New York I'll call you for your answer. Have a safe flight, Andrea."

"You, too," she whispered before walking back to the hotel alone.

The rest of the morning passed in a blur as a limo pulled up in front of the hotel and swept her away to the airport. Evidently yesterday's romantic raft ride across the river was all part of the atmosphere he'd orchestrated to prove she wasn't physically indifferent to him. Her enthusiastic response to him on the dance floor had probably shocked him.

Six hours later she stepped off his private jet where she discovered his driver waiting for her. "Welcome back, Ms. Bauer."

"Good morning, Benny."

"Mr. Corbin said you haven't had much sleep after such a short trip. He told me to take you straight to your apartment."

Nothing escaped Gabe's notice. "I have to admit I'm tired. Thank you for coming to get me."

"It's a pleasure." He helped her in the back of the limo before they drove into Manhattan.

There weren't many clouds overhead. It didn't look anything like the sky above Champigny. She couldn't smell the perfume in the air. The atmosphere was all wrong.

Everything was wrong because Gabe wasn't with her…

When she entertained the thought of never seeing him again, an emptiness stole through her too terrible to contemplate.

"Here we are, Ms. Bauer," Benny said twenty minutes later. He'd come around to open her door. She'd been so buried in thought, she hadn't realized they were back in front of her apartment.

Andrea climbed out and thanked him for the ride.

He handed her the suitcase. "I'm always glad to be of service."

She waved him off and hurried inside.

One of the first things she did after entering her small fourth floor apartment was go to the kitchen and listen to the messages on her answering machine.

There were several calls from her mom wondering if she'd be coming home for the weekend. Sue, a friend in the same apartment building, wanted to go to lunch. The next voice was Bret's.

"It was hard seeing you at the elevator without being able to talk. I'm missing you like crazy, Andrea. Forgive me for accusing you of being in love with the boss. You said you weren't, but I wouldn't listen. Maybe it's because I sensed his interest in you from the beginning."

She shook her head. Bret was so wrong where Gabe was concerned.

"I'll admit I've been jealous as hell. Gabe Corbin is an impossible act for the normal man to compete with. Can we start over again? If I promise not—"

Andrea deleted all the messages, too torn up over the decision she was grappling with to deal with anything else. She'd heard of people who said they'd reached a turning point in their life that had altered it forever. It never occurred to her she would be one of those people.

While she stood there trying to sort out her chaotic emotions, her cell phone rang. She reached in her purse for it.

The caller ID indicated an out of area call. It was probably her mom. She clicked on. "Hello?"

"I'm glad you arrived safely, Andrea."

Gabe— She clung to the edge of the counter for support.

"You've had seven hours to consider my proposal. I'd like your answer now."

Now?

The phone fell to the floor. She rushed to retrieve it. Her hand pressed against her heart where it pounded so hard, it hurt. She hadn't expected to hear from him until tonight.

"A-are you still in Paris?" she spluttered.

She felt his hesitation before he said, "I'm at the airport. If you've decided to marry me, we have plans to make. Otherwise I'm going to fly to St. Pierre now."

The breath froze in her lungs. "H-how long will you be there?"

"For good. I thought you understood that."

"But—"

"It sounds like you've made your decision," he interrupted without missing a beat. "Andrea, I thought my proposition would make you happy, that it would give you one last chance at getting pregnant. But I understand your decision—and I hope your surgery is successful and you'll be pain-free.

"Don't worry about anything at the office. I'll phone Sam Poon and let him decide how to reorganize your department. You can pick up your severance pay-check from Karen."

"Wait—!" she cried out in panic.

"If you're uncertain about quitting, so much the better for the company, Andrea. Take your six weeks to recover. By then you may feel diff—"

"No—" This time it was she who cut *him* off.

"No, what?"

The blood pounded in her ears. "You've misunderstood me. I—I want to try to have a baby."

"That's all I needed to hear." Gabe sounded quietly pleased, just like he did when he'd sewn up another market on the international scene. "I'll meet you at the county clerk's office at three. Benny will be by for you at two-thirty. See you then, Andrea."

He clicked off before she could say goodbye.

Dear God... What had she done? She could hear her mother's voice asking her the same question.

The more she thought about it, the more Andrea feared calling her parents. Gabe wasn't in love with her. Better for them not to know anything yet.

There was every possibility she wouldn't be making that three o'clock deadline downtown Gabe had set...

CHAPTER THREE

BAUER'S Eidelweiss Chalet formed part of a strip mall in Scarsdale that might as well have been one of those wonderful little shops nestled in the heart of Germany's Black Forest.

Gabe entered the virtual fairyland just as a cuckoo went off twelve times announcing the noon hour. Every conceivable kind of hand-painted wood nutcracker and doll house covered the display tables. On one side of the shop were Christmas ornaments, music boxes, smokers, steins and cowbells. The other side sold Bavarian clothing.

He glimpsed Andrea's dark-blond father dressed in traditional lederhosen up on a ladder. The tall, fit man with a short beard and moustache was setting up a crèche pyramid. Her mother had to be the attractive brunette woman behind the counter dressed in a Bavarian blue dirndl.

Andrea's parents looked to be in their mid-fifties. Both appeared to be the picture of perfect health, which made fiction out of Andrea's insistence that they were getting old and needed her help.

She'd inherited traits from both of them, particularly her mother who had those same bluebell colored eyes and a healthy bloom on her cheeks. The well-endowed Bauer women wore little makeup. They didn't need to with such flawless skin.

He waited until their only customer left the store, then he approached the counter. "Renate Bauer?"

"Yes?" She eyed him as if she were trying to remember if she'd seen him before.

"I'm Gabe Corbin, Andrea's employer."

The second she recognized his name, a look of anxiety replaced her friendly smile. Her complexion paled.

"Karl!" she cried to her husband. "Come quick! Mr. Corbin's here. Something must have happened to our dau—"

"Andrea's fine!" Gabe rushed to assure her before any more damage was done. By now her husband had joined them. "I'm sorry if our first meeting has led you to believe I'm the bearer of bad news. Nothing could be further from the truth."

Relief slowly chased away their alarmed expressions.

"Andrea and I just returned from Paris. While we were there, I asked her to be my wife and she accepted. I would have come to you first to ask for her hand, but circumstances made it impossible."

They both stared at him incredulously before her mother said, "Excuse me while I put the Closed sign in the window."

While she hurried to do that, her husband recovered enough to hold out his hand and shake Gabe's. "You're all my daughter has talked about for the last six months, but she never let on that your relationship had become personal."

That was the best news Gabe had heard in a long time. By now Mrs. Bauer had returned.

"When I promoted Andrea four months ago, I

learned she was dating someone else in the company. I had to wait until the field was free of competition before I made my move."

Her mother looked happy, and yet— "Where is she?"

"My driver dropped her off at her apartment."

"That's odd. I've left messages, but she hasn't returned them."

Gabe could have enlightened her that her daughter was in a state of shock and on the verge of changing her mind at any second.

"We're meeting at the county clerk's office at three to get our license. No doubt she has a lot to do between now and then." He cleared his throat. "Andrea has no idea I'm here. I came because I wanted to talk to you about her endometriosis."

Renate leaned against her husband with a sigh. "We're glad you know about that."

"She has suffered a lot," Karl murmured.

"I know. Andrea only told me about her condition recently. Since there are only six months left before she has to have the hysterectomy, we don't have time to plan a big wedding.

"We need to take advantage of every moment left to us. That's why I'd like us to be married today, but only if you can be there with us."

Her parents looked at each other with dazed expressions.

"A friend of mine, Judge Rivers of the appellate court, is standing by. He'll waive the twenty-four-hour waiting period."

Renate's eyes filled. "I think it's romantic and wonderful."

Karl studied Gabe for a long moment. "Our daughter has a sensible head on her shoulders. If she's chosen you for her husband, that's good enough for us."

"Welcome to the family, Gabe," Renate cried before hugging him.

"Thank you," he murmured, humbled by their acceptance of him when all they had to go on was their faith in Andrea. "Could I ask you another favor?"

"Of course," she said, wiping her eyes.

"How would you feel if Andrea and I came back here after the ceremony and spent a week with you? I'd like to get to know my in-laws, and I know nothing would make Andrea happier."

"Nothing would make us happier." Karl's voice had gone husky. "Come on, Renate. We've got to go home and get ready for a wedding."

"I'll drive you," Gabe offered. "I'll tell you our plans en route. You need to know we won't be living in New York..."

"Ms. Bauer? I'm out in front."

"Thanks for the call, Benny. I'll be right down."

It would be cowardly to make him the messenger. All Andrea had to do was show up at the clerk's office and tell Gabe she'd changed her mind about getting married.

He wasn't in love with her. As much as she wanted to conceive before it was too late, without love on both sides, their marriage couldn't possibly work.

If she did have a baby, it wouldn't be fair to raise it in a home where the parents weren't crazy about each other. Look what had happened to Gabe's parents!

By the time Benny had deposited her in front of the municipal court building at five after three, she'd memorized her speech and was prepared to deliver it.

The signs with arrows made it easy to find the marriage license bureau on the first floor. In the crowded room she was looking so hard for Gabe, she passed right by her parents before coming to a standstill. Stunned, she whirled around, wondering if she were hallucinating. But no. There they were, all dressed up and smiling at her.

"Mom? Dad? What are you doing here?"

Her mother embraced her first. "Congratulations, darling. Between you and me, I think Gabe Corbin is the most exciting, handsome man I've ever met in my life. Besides your father of course."

In the next breath her dad was squeezing her. "I approve of him, Andrea. He's going to make you a fine husband. Taking you home to St. Pierre to live and work with his family means he's got his priorities straight. I admire that in a man who's been as successful as he is. Come on. Let's go."

"Wait—" she cried. "I was supposed to meet him here to get a license!"

I was going to tell him I can't go through with this after all.

"We know," her mom said. "But he's anxious to marry you now because of your condition. Luckily he was able to arrange for a ceremony with the judge who's a friend of his. The man is already late for court so we have to hurry. They're upstairs waiting for you."

Her parents rushed her along to the elevator. Andrea was so dazed by the fact that he'd already been in touch with her parents, she hardly knew which foot to put in front of the other.

"This is all happening too fast, Mom."

"You've been in love with him since the day you went to work for him, darling. It's the reason why no other man has interested you."

"Yes, I know, bu—"

"Then don't worry about disappointing your father and me because you think you're cheating us out of a big wedding," her mother reasoned. "If Gabe's ever going to have a baby with you, it's got to happen in the next six months.

"I don't blame him for being in a hurry. Sometimes it takes months to conceive. You two are running out of time. Your father and I have made it no secret we're looking forward to being grandparents."

"Mom—you don't und—"

She never got to finish the rest of her sentence because Gabe was standing there bigger than life as the doors opened on the next floor. His eyes gleamed silver as they captured hers. For the life of her, she couldn't think, couldn't make a sound.

He was dressed in a formal slate suit with a dazzling white shirt and silk striped tie. In his lapel he wore a small gardenia. *The ultimate bridegroom.*

His hands held a larger gardenia for her. Her heart fluttered like a pennant in the wind.

"Gabe—" she whispered in a shaky voice.

"It's still not too late to change your mind," he whispered back, biting her earlobe gently. It sent a hot sensation through her sensitized body. Before she could breathe, he'd pinned the flowers to the shoulder of the eggshell colored blouse she'd worn with the pants of her tan pantsuit.

She moaned. "I can't get married looking like this!"

He slid his arm around her, drawing her tightly against him. "You look lovely in anything you wear. Just put your signature on the marriage license and Judge Rivers will begin the ceremony.

"Your parents have offered to be our witnesses. I like them very much, Andrea," he confided in his deep voice.

It was hard to swallow. "None of *your* family is here—" she lamented. A clerk distracted her by handing her a pen so she could sign the license.

"I tried to reach my mother but she wasn't home. As for my father, he'll find out soon enough when we arrive on the island." Gabe's eyes darkened. "You're going to be my family now. That's all that matters."

"No it isn't, and you know it!"

"Ms. Bauer? I'm Judge Rivers."

The impressive looking gray-haired man in black robes stepped forward to shake her hand.

"H-how do you do."

"It's a pleasure to meet the woman who has brought Gabe to his senses at last. If your parents will stand on your right while the two of you clasp hands, we'll begin."

She felt Gabe's fingers interlock with hers in a firm grip. His physical warmth told her this was no dream. They were really getting married!

The judge stood with his legs slightly apart. "Two people who've worked in the same company together might know a lot about each other. But you never really find out what another person is like until you've lived with them in the bonds of marriage.

"I'm pleased Gabe wants to marry you rather than simply live with you as so many couples are wont to do. It means that no matter what the future may hold, he believes in forever and isn't afraid to make a commitment before God and man.

"It also means he intends to take care of your every need, not only the physical love which is vitally important, but certainly not the sum total of a relationship which I believe is ordained of God.

"I'm pleased Andrea wants to enter into the marriage covenant, to be your helpmate and your comfort. Her commitment means the bearing and raising of children if you are so blessed." Upon those words, Gabe tightened his hold.

"Though the dark times will come as Mr. and Mrs. Bauer will attest, they're always followed by better times because you've lived by faith to sustain you, making your marriage stronger and more beautiful with each challenge.

"Andrea Bauer, do you take Gabriel Corbin to be your lawfully wedded husband? Do you promise to love, honor, cherish and remain true to him until death do you part?"

She had this suffocating feeling in her chest. The judge could have no idea this marriage was starting out on faith and nothing else! "I—I do."

"Gabriel Corbin, do you take Andrea Bauer to be your lawfully wedded wife? Do you promise to love, honor, cherish and remain true to her until death to you part?"

"I do," came Gabe's solemn response.

"Then by the power invested in me by the State of New York, I pronounce you husband and wife. If you have rings, you may exchange them now."

Gabe reached in his pocket and slid home a solid gold band on the ring finger of her left hand. She had nothing to give him.

When she looked up, he must have read her mind because he said, "Don't worry about it. I've got *you*."

"I'm late for court, Gabe. Hurry and kiss your lovely bride. This is the part I like best."

Andrea's father chuckled.

Gabe smiled down at her. "Me, too," he teased before carrying out the judge's order.

As a wedding kiss, it was all she could have dreamed of. Long, ardent and passionate enough to convince everyone theirs was a great love match.

When Gabe finally relinquished her trembling mouth the judge said, "May I be the first to congratulate you, Mrs. Corbin."

Mrs. Corbin.

Less than twenty-four hours ago Andrea had approached Gabe about leaving his employ. Now he was her husband! Things like this just didn't happen in real life!

"Thank you, Judge Rivers."

After kissing her cheek, he shook hands with her parents. While Gabe walked him to the door, her mom and dad took turns hugging her. The whole scene was surreal.

When the older man had left the room, Gabe retraced his steps and put his arm around her waist. "I don't know about you, Mrs. Corbin, but I'm ready to leave on our honeymoon."

Andrea was powerless to stop the blush that stained her throat and cheeks. "Where are we going?"

"To our house," her mother exclaimed in delight.

Her father nodded. "Gabe said he was willing to share you for the next week. I like my new son-in-law already."

Of course you do.

There was no man in the world who could ever measure up to Gabe. To her sorrow it was equally true that his heart had died of pain a long time ago. No woman on earth had the power to bring it back to life.

But a baby would give him a whole new reason to live... *His* baby...

If she kept that thought uppermost in her mind, she just might make it through her wedding night.

The evening was warm and humid. Andrea lost the battle with fatigue and closed her eyes. She could hear everyone talking while they sat out on her parents' veranda, but she'd lost the thread of the conversation.

"Your daughter's ready to pass out on me, Karl. I think it's time for bed."

"After two transatlantic flights back-to-back and a wedding, I'm not surprised," Andrea's father murmured.

Gabe got up from the swing and drew her along with him. When she weaved on her feet, he put his strong arms around her waist to support her. But all that managed to do was send a quivery sensation through her body making her more unsteady than ever.

"Renate? Thank you for dinner, that was the best Wiener schnitzel I've ever tasted."

"Thank you. It's a family recipe. Andrea knows how to make it."

Her dad stood up. "We'll go into the shop in the morning and come back to have a late lunch with you."

"We'll look forward to that," Gabe said as his lips brushed Andrea's temple. "Come on, darling. You'll have to show me the way."

Darling— He couldn't have said anything to bring her more fully awake.

"Good night," she murmured to her parents and pulled out of his arms. Without waiting for him, she walked through the two-story colonial and marched up the stairs.

On the way home from the courthouse, Gabe had driven them by her apartment so she could pack a few things. He'd already packed his case before he'd gone to see her parents.

Everything had been taken care of. Nothing had been left to chance. That was the way Gabe operated. Already her parents adored him.

But once he'd followed her into her old bedroom and they were on her turf, she wheeled around determined to set some ground rules. To her chagrin he was standing so close, she had to back away from him. His overwhelming masculine physique dwarfed her bedroom which had never seen another man in it besides her father.

It was silly, but she started to panic. "We both know the underlying reason for this marriage," she began, "so I would appreciate it if you wouldn't call me darling again."

He stared at her through shuttered eyes. "What else?"

She moistened her lips nervously. "What do you mean?"

"Give me the whole list of 'don't's' right now. I'll try my best to honor your wishes."

He was being so reasonable she couldn't think of anything else to say. That in itself made her want to throw something at him.

"Andrea— I'm aware you've never made love before. Though I may be your husband, I swear I won't do anything you don't want me to do. Frankly I'm as exhausted as you are and need a good night's sleep.

"If you don't mind, I'll get ready for bed first. You come when you're ready."

She watched helplessly as he disappeared into her bathroom.

Instead of being relieved, she was hurt that he didn't desire her enough to try to seduce her like he'd done in Champigny. After his all-fired rush to get married, he'd just let her know there wasn't going to be a wedding night because he was too tired!

Since she didn't want her parents to know anything was wrong, she didn't dare slip down the hall to the guest bathroom. Worse, she didn't want Gabe to emerge and discover her standing there with the gardenias still pinned to her blouse like she was some terrified virgin afraid to breathe.

While she could hear the shower running, she changed into her nightgown and robe, then sat at the dressing table to brush her hair. But that seemed an equally ridiculous pretense.

She was a mature, twenty-eight-year-old woman for heaven's sake!

After throwing her robe on the end of the bed, she turned out the light and slipped under the covers. Let him think what he wanted when he discovered she'd gone to sleep before he had.

Two minutes later she felt his presence at her side of the bed. The light went on. When she opened her eyes, there was Gabe, smooth shaven, wearing the bottom half of a pair of pajamas and nothing else.

The hair on his well-defined chest was as black as it was everywhere else. She was so bemused at the sight of his superb body she hardly noticed he held a small box in his hands that could be a jewelry case.

Was he about to give her a wedding present?

He sat down next to her and opened it. The smell of the soap he'd used in the shower assailed her senses, distracting her.

"I bought this basal body thermometer so you can start taking your temperature every morning before you get out of bed." He put it on her nightstand. "There's a graph inside the case to keep a record.

"I also bought a couple of fertility kits. The pharmacist told me you need two for the month. They're the latest thing. I left them in the bathroom for you."

Her first thought was that Gabe couldn't have found the time to do all this and remain in Paris long after she'd left.

His solemn gaze sought hers. "Don't hate me too much, Andrea." His voice grated. "If you don't know it already, I'm a man who doesn't like to leave anything to chance if I can help it. Certainly not the time period when I can get you pregnant."

As he started to get up she checked his movement with her hand. "I could never hate you, Gabe. I know you're doing this for both of us. If anything, I'm grateful to you for making this easier for me."

A tiny nerve throbbed at the corner of his sensuous mouth, but she couldn't tell what he was thinking.

"When's your next period?"

"In about two and a half weeks, provided I'm regular. Sometimes I'm not."

His eyes turned to quicksilver. "That means we've got a chance this month." He leaned over and gave her a chaste kiss on the lips. "Sleep well. Tomorrow morning we'll both feel like new people."

New people?

She was a brand-new bride! You didn't get any newer than that!

Suddenly the room was shrouded in darkness. The mattress gave on Gabe's side. It didn't take long before she could tell by the rhythm of his breathing that he'd fallen asleep.

After sleeping alone for twenty-eight years, it should have felt strange to have anyone else in bed with her. But this was Gabe, the man she adored. To know he was within touching distance of her... All she had to do was roll over to find herself in the arms of her new husband.

For the next ten minutes a battle raged inside her whether she should take the initiative and wake him up. In the end she couldn't find the courage, and decided a shower might help her to unwind.

As she started to slide out of bed, a powerful arm snaked around her waist. "Oh—" she gasped as he drew her against his hard-muscled frame. Her heart skidded out of control. "I—I didn't mean to waken you, Gabe."

He kissed her nape, filling her system with shooting stars. "I couldn't sleep any more than you could. If you knew me better, you'd realize it would be impossible for me to lie next to you without wanting to make love to you."

It was sheer revelation to feel his hands wander over her body, awakening needs she didn't know she had. Her breathing grew ragged.

"You're a totally feminine, desirable woman. Getting you pregnant is without a doubt the most delightful task I've ever undertaken."

Before she knew how it had happened, he'd turned her so she was facing him. By now their bodies and legs were entwined.

"You don't need to be afraid to look at me, Andrea. Neither of us smells of garlic tonight."

His comment drew a shaky laugh from her which he quieted with his lips. Then everything changed because he began kissing her with primitive urgency.

His hungry mouth explored the classic contours of her face, neck and shoulders, her honey silk hair. Each time he returned to her mouth, it was as if he were starving for her and couldn't get enough.

Neither could Andrea who'd been on fire for him since Paris, and felt every inhibition vanish. She knew he didn't love her, but they both wanted a baby so badly, nothing seemed more important than giving each other pleasure that would result in one.

As time wore on, that pleasure became ecstasy almost beyond bearing. She experienced it over and over again as he made love to her several times throughout the night. At some point they finally slept.

As sunlight filtered through the window, Gabe had the presence of mind to waken her.

His slumberous gaze played over her features. "Good morning, Mrs. Corbin," he said in a voice that sounded an octave lower than usual. "Time to take your temperature."

In a half drugged state she put the thermometer in her mouth while he left her long enough to shave. When he'd returned and recorded her temperature, he slid beneath the covers and started caressing her arm with growing insistence as a prelude to making love.

Eager to know that rapture again, Andrea sought his mouth with a hunger she didn't try to hide. This time she wanted to bring him the same joy he brought her. They made glorious love until they were temporarily sated and fell back to sleep once more.

The next time Andrea was cognizant of Gabe's arm wrapped possessively around her hip, she realized she'd been wakened by the sound of her parents' car pulling into the driveway.

She glanced at her watch. Five to two.

Her face went hot when she realized she and Gabe had been in bed over sixteen hours!

"Gabe—we've got to get up. Mom and Dad are home."

He pulled her on top of him and cupped her flushed cheeks in his hands. "Relax. They know we're trying for a baby."

With those words, the little glimmer of hope that had been growing inside Andrea throughout the night because she thought maybe Gabe's emotions were involved, flickered and died.

After the ecstasy she'd experienced in his arms, she'd almost forgotten why her husband had been such an enthusiastic lover.

Like those moments on the dance floor in Champigny, had he also scripted everything that had happened throughout their wedding night? Even those groans of satisfaction deep in his throat? Had they been orchestrated to make her think she'd satisfied him, too?

Andrea had known there'd be a price to pay for loving a man who didn't love her. In her naiveté she hadn't realized the physical act of making love would be so beautiful that without Gabe's love behind it, the pain would crucify her.

"Where do you think you're going?" She'd heard that silken voice during the night and scrambled out of his arms to reach for her robe. She found it lying on the floor. It must have fallen off the bed during the night. She had no idea where her nightgown was hiding.

She cinched the tie around her waist. "Even a man doing his duty needs to stop for food. I'm going to do mine and fix you lunch."

He lay in the bed like a dark-haired god, taunting her with his seductive half smile. "Make it a big one then. You've given me a huge appetite."

When she entered the bathroom, she saw the two fertility kits sitting on the counter, more evidence of Gabe's desperate need to father a child.

Tears burned her eyes.

No doubt a baby would fill an empty place inside him, but it could never erase Gabe's guilt.

If all these years Yves had assumed Jeanne-Marie had lost *their* baby, then it wasn't Yves or Jeanne-Marie Gabe feared. That left his father...

Did Gabe hope to win back a little of his dad's approval by returning to the island with a wife and hope of a child in the near future?

Was that why Gabe was giving away his fortune? To earn his father's respect?

No son should have to do that!

Family relationships were always complicated. Due to the fact that they all lived on the island in a close community, she imagined the dynamics in the Corbin household where a divorce had taken place were particularly convoluted.

And what about his mother? What part did she play in his guilt? Did she know the secret, too? Was she aware of how much Gabe had suffered? Had she encouraged him to stay away from the family to make sure there was no scandal?

Gabe had warned Andrea his family might never accept her. When she'd been so upset because not one member of his family had been present at the courthouse, he'd told her she was the only family he needed.

But that wasn't true—otherwise he wouldn't be turning his back on the empire he'd built to return to his roots like the prodigal son needing his father's forgiveness and love.

Andrea buried her wet face in the nearest towel. She didn't know how he'd survived without both all these years.

She'd never felt so helpless in all her life.

CHAPTER FOUR

TEN days later Andrea found herself high above the earth once more, her heart pounding with anxiety. Instead of being on a business trip with her boss in his private jet, she was traveling with her new husband on a passenger plane from Halifax. They were headed toward unfriendly territory and an unknown future as man and wife.

While they'd used her parents' as a home base, Gabe had made frequent trips into Manhattan to divest himself of his assets and arrange for a realtor to sell their apartments. The few belongings they'd wanted to keep would be shipped to the island at a later date.

She didn't question why Gabe had chosen for them to arrive on the island like normal tourists. Of course there was nothing normal about him. He'd given his worldly riches for the betterment of his family and the island. But his father and brothers didn't know that. Perhaps they never would.

The Corbins of St. Pierre et Miquelon, along with their acquaintances, were only cognizant of one truth; Gabe had done the unforgivable by leaving the island years ago to make his fortune in the computer business.

After all this time, Andrea more than anyone understood why he didn't want to return like the billionaire VIP he was, flaunting his possessions and wealth in their faces.

The long estrangement from his family hadn't been of his making. Still, if he hoped to repair the damage, every move he contemplated from this point on had to be thought out with reconciliation uppermost in his mind. That was one area where Andrea intended to help in any way she could.

Though her parents didn't know every detail of Gabe's tragic past, she'd told them about his family's resentment of him for leaving home, and the uphill battle facing them once they reached the island. To learn of the pain he'd lived with all these years brought out their compassionate instincts.

After spending all this time with Gabe, her mom and dad thought the world of him. They urged Andrea to stand by him no matter how difficult the situation might become.

She didn't need to be told that, but she loved them for being protective of him and caring as much as they did.

In ten days all their lives had been transformed by the remarkable man who'd become a husband and son-in-law, making him an intrinsic part of the Bauer family.

Certainly Andrea wasn't the same employee who'd gone to her boss in the depths of despair because she was facing an operation that would crush her dream to give birth to her own baby. That person was no-where to be found.

In her stead was a woman who was so madly in love with her husband, she could hardly breathe just sitting next to him on the plane, anticipating the night to come when he would pull her into his arms.

She couldn't imagine a lover being more attentive

and exciting. Yet always in the back of her mind was the knowledge that this exercise in passion was meant to make her believe she was loved. In that state, conception had the greatest chance of occurring.

No matter how carried away she was by the rapture he created, Gabe never failed to hand her the thermometer at the same time every morning, reminding her what their nights of connubial bliss were really all about.

In the broad light of day, the realization of that truth hurt to the depths of her being. Yet by the time the sun went down, she always found herself counting the minutes until Gabe suggested they say good-night to her parents and go to bed.

But tonight would be different from the others because they would be spending them with Gabe's grandfather. She feared Gabe was going to be a very different person now. In her heart she knew everything was about to change, and it terrified her.

Though Gabe had assured her his grandfather would accept Andrea without question, she couldn't pretend that it was going to be love at first sight.

Andrea wasn't a French girl from the island, and she didn't speak his native tongue. In fact with her computer engineering degree, she was the antithesis of the kind of woman the Corbin men chose to marry. *Except for Gabe's mother.*

That's what made everything worse.

Gabe's family would take one look at Andrea and assume it was only a matter of time before history repeated itself and she left for the mainland because she couldn't take the harsh life.

"We're approaching the islands, Andrea," Gabe murmured near her ear.

A nuance of intense emotion accompanied his words. She felt the tautening of his body though they weren't actually touching.

What might be a fascinating scenic attraction to someone else represented home to her husband. A home he'd been exiled from for eighteen years because Gabe had chosen to honor his father's autocratic wishes.

As she looked out the window of the plane, the cruelty he'd inflicted on his son seemed to reassert itself, killing Andrea's heart all over again as surely as if someone had driven a lance through it. Biting her lip, she tried to concentrate on the view.

Against a summer-blue sky, small dots of clouds sat like cotton tufts on invisible shelves. Gabe had told her there were seven islands, but all she could count from her angle in the seat were three land masses surrounded by the cobalt-hued waters of the North Atlantic. Thousands of miles to the east lay the coast of France, their mother country.

Gabe had grown up here, a son of the sea. Like Ulysses hearing the song of the Sirens, he was being lured to treacherous shores that looked incredibly benign from this altitude. But no one knew the outcome.

Andrea shivered with apprehension for this new chapter of pain about to unfold in her husband's life. If she could prevent him from being hurt again, she would do it. But of course that wasn't possible.

A strong, warm masculine hand clasped hers. "Grand-père's going to be very taken with you, Andrea."

What an irony Gabe was attempting to comfort her when it should be the other way around. She sucked in her breath. "I hope so."

"After we land, we'll take a taxi to his house. On a beautiful June afternoon like this, he's probably out fishing. It'll give us time to get settled before he returns."

"It might shock him too much to discover we're there."

"No."

"Gabe— Don't you think—"

"Don't worry," he silenced her. "Grand-père has waited a long time for this day. He hasn't been able to predict the exact hour, but he has known it was coming. Just as I have," he added in a gravelly voice full of long suppressed emotion. It moved her to tears.

To her relief the Fasten Seat Belt warning began flashing. Andrea averted her eyes to buckle up before looking out the window once more. Closer now the beautiful archipelago unfolded to her fascinated gaze.

Strange to think that only twenty-five miles from the coast of Newfoundland, you were in France.

She glimpsed Saint-Pierre, the capital city of 6,800 people bordering a natural port with a picturesque bay. Beyond it the greater part of the island appeared to be made up of rocky hills.

As the plane started its descent, the colors of the buildings and houses ranging from gold to blue and green leaped up to greet her, delighting the eye. She couldn't imagine a less dreary place, but then she hadn't experienced winter here yet.

Most of the passengers who deboarded with them were French teachers from the U.S. coming for a language conference. In the rest room at the Halifax airport Andrea had met one of the women teachers from Madison, Wisconsin, named Marsha Evans who'd told her about it.

Like Andrea, neither she nor the other teachers had ever been to St. Pierre et Miquelon before. While Andrea and Gabe waited for their luggage, she could hear their excitement in being able to read the signs and exchange their dollars for French francs or Euro dollars. All of them tried out their French. Some did better than others.

Compared to her husband, they had a long way to go to sound like native speakers. That was another area Andrea intended to work on.

Her parents had insisted she take six years of German throughout junior and senior high so she could converse with her relatives when they traveled to Heidelberg every summer.

If she ever hoped to fit in with Gabe's family, she would have to learn to speak their native tongue to gain favor with them.

"Shall we go?" Gabe suggested once they'd removed their suitcases from the carousel. He dealt with the three heaviest ones while she carried her shoulder bag and overnight case. Together they left the terminal and walked out to the parking area where there were several taxis and a bus waiting.

One chauffeur de taxi with dark brown hair who looked to be about Gabe's age had been lounging against the door enjoying a cigarette. That was until he eyed Gabe, then the cigarette fell from his lips.

"Gabriel Corbin?" he called out before walking toward them. *"C'est vraiment toi?"*

"Oui, Fabrice. C'est moi."

"Incroyable!"

The other man with the broad forehead broke out in a huge smile and reached for Andrea's husband, heartily embracing him, kissing him on both cheeks. Her spirits lifted to realize not everyone in St. Pierre had turned their backs on him.

After they'd conversed for a moment in rapid-fire French Gabe turned to her. *"Mon coeur,"* he said before switching to English, "meet Fabrice Palmentier, my best friend before I left the island. We got into a lot of trouble together. Fabrice? This is my wife, Andrea."

"How do you do." She shook hands with the shorter man who studied her with frank male admiration. Eventually his gaze flicked to Gabe. "If you'd stayed here, *mon ami,* you would never have found someone like her. Now that I've met the woman who has stolen your heart, I forgive you for your absence."

I haven't stolen his heart, Fabrice. Far from it.

"How long are you going to be here? Lise always preferred you to me, and won't forgive me if I don't get you over to the house for dinner."

Such an innocent remark probably held a kernel of truth. It came as no surprise to Andrea that her husband had been a heartbreaker.

"There's nothing my wife and I would like more. After we're settled in our house, we'll want to reciprocate."

Fabrice's head reared back. "What house?"

"I bought the one next to Grand-père's. We'll stay with him until it's ready to move into."

Shock rendered him immobile.

"You're joking, *n'est-ce pas?*" he whispered.

"*Non, mon vieux.* I'm back home for good."

If Andrea wasn't mistaken, Fabrice's brown eyes held a suspicious brightness. Suddenly he started to laugh, then he was giving Gabe a bear hug, the kind Andrea's father gave her when he was too happy to talk. It caught the attention of the teacher Andrea had met. She waved to Andrea before climbing on the bus with the others.

The look of relief on Gabe's face as he hugged his friend back gave her deeper insight into her husband's psyche. He'd honestly thought that life from here on out was going to be a case of the two of them against the world.

But now he had proof that wasn't true. His friend had always been in his corner. Though she couldn't do it yet, one day when Andrea knew Fabrice better, she would hug him and let him know what his heart-felt welcome had meant to her husband. He could have no idea looking at Gabe that her husband had arrived on the island at his lowest ebb.

He badly needed an ally. Who better than his best buddy from the past? Andrea had the impression Gabe's departure from St. Pierre years ago had been hard on a lot of people, including Fabrice.

Meeting him by accident like this today of all days was a wonderful omen.

"Come," Fabrice said, grabbing two of the bags. "I'll drive you to the house. It will be like old times."

Andrea could hear his affection for Gabe. Though her husband wasn't normally as demonstrative with other people, she sensed changes in him now.

Once they were both seated in the back of the taxi,

his body didn't feel as tense against hers. While Fabrice drove through the town to a residential area maybe four miles from the center, Gabe bantered back and forth in French with him the way they'd probably done in their early school days.

From the grins and grunts and male laughter, she knew they were reminiscing about things only the two of them could share. If anyone in Gabe's financial empire could see him like this, they wouldn't recognize him. For the moment he'd shed that remote, brooding expression. To Andrea he seemed years younger all of a sudden and carefree.

She would sell her soul to make this last...

When Andrea could finally break in on their conversation, she asked Fabrice how many children he had.

"Two and a half," he called over his shoulder.

Gabe had been holding her hand. At Fabrice's answer, he rubbed his thumb over her palm in a sensual caress that set her trembling. Whether intentional or not, she knew he was thinking about the baby they were trying to have.

But now that he was back in St. Pierre, she feared memories of the night he'd spent with Jeanne-Marie when he'd gotten her pregnant would start to plague him more forcefully. Andrea didn't even want to think what it was going to be like when he saw her again, especially since she was Yves's wife on top of being Gabe's former girlfriend.

In front of his brother, Gabe would have to be the consummate actor, never letting on that Jeanne-Marie had anything to do with the reason he'd stayed away from St. Pierre all these years. No one in his family would ever know how infinite his suffering had been.

She stared out the window at the cluster of houses built close to each other in many different shapes and sizes. It was tragic to think of Gabe's relatives living here in a remote area of the world all this time, yet his father had never broken down and asked him to come home, not even for a visit.

"How does it feel to be back, *mon ami?*"

"Not much has changed, Fabrice."

Andrea thought everything looked neat and clean. There were few trees, quite a lot of cars and several huge white satellite dishes.

Fabrice turned down another road paralleling the water's edge. Obviously they had come to one end of the island which was mostly hill covered with low growing vegetation. Only a few houses were in this section facing the ocean where you could see several stone jetties with all kinds of boats moored.

He pulled up in front of two houses grouped together. One of them was a charming two-story with blue siding and white trim whose shape reminded her of a Swiss chalet. You had to climb stairs to reach the porch. Several tall pines grew near one corner and shrubbery surrounded the base.

Next to the pines sat the other two-story wooden structure in what Andrea considered a sick pink with gray trim and a dark lavender-pink base set on wood pilings. Its style resembled one of those lonely country churches you might see out on the prairie. Her eyes took in the long rectangle with the tall pitched roof. Instead of a belfry there was a window.

"One man's junk is another man's treasure. We'll

paint it another color and put in some landscaping after we take possession,'' Gabe said in a low voice against her ear before kissing her temple.

Andrea might have known. Her mouth curved upward. ''It's going to need some work all right.''

''I'm looking forward to it.''

He sounded like he meant it. The kind of hands-on remodeling he was talking about had no place in the fast paced corporate world of high finance and computers where he'd been living all this time.

The two of them might just as well have arrived from another planet. Andrea still felt she was wandering in a strange land she could never have conjured in a hundred years.

''When you went to New York on your own, you must have felt a little like Saint-Exupéry's *petit prince*. No more volcanoes to sweep out, no little flower to water.''

She heard his breath escape. ''How do you do that, Andrea?''

''What do you mean?''

''It's uncanny the way you pick up on my thoughts at times, like now.''

His comment thrilled her because she felt it was honest, and not a part of the playacting he did every night.

''Jacques has come out on the porch,'' Fabrice informed Gabe. ''Let me help you with the bags. I want to say hello to him.''

Gabe had already spotted his grandfather's ancient fishing boat tied up at the jetty and realized he was probably inside the house.

A lump lodged in his throat as he looked out the window at him standing there waving to Fabrice in his typical dark pants and pullover.

Any black that had been in his hair two years ago had gone gray. Even from the distance separating them it was apparent his weathered face had more lines, but his wiry body seemed active as ever. He descended the stairs with the agility of a man ten years younger.

"Don't worry about me, Gabe," Andrea said, practically pushing him out the door of Fabrice's taxi. "Go greet him!"

He squeezed her hand before levering himself from the back seat.

"Gabriel—" he heard his grandfather cry before they reached each other. Gabe wrapped his arms around the old man, noticing he'd lost an inch or two and was thinner than he should be.

"I'm home to stay, Grand-père," he said in a husky voice, kissing him on both cheeks several times.

His grandfather wept openly. *"Dieu merci, Dieu merci."*

"I've brought someone with me." He turned to Andrea who was standing next to Fabrice. Illuminated by the slanting rays of the sun, her moist blue eyes looked like jewels. They mesmerized him.

He put his arm around her waist. "Grand-père? Meet my wife, Andrea Bauer. Andrea—this is my grandfather, Jean-Jacques Corbin, but everyone calls him Jacques."

Normally Gabe's grandfather was a little more verbal, but for once he couldn't seem to find words. Gabe could tell that he wasn't only charmed by Andrea's natural golden looks, he was moved by the emotion she couldn't hide.

Her soul reflected in her warm smile, touching Gabe in places he hadn't been aware of. "I've wanted to meet you for a long time, Monsieur Corbin."

"The wife of my grandson must call me Jacques!" he declared in a scolding voice. *"Tu compris?"*

She nodded.

"Bon. Sois la bien venue, ma fille."

His grandfather kissed her on both cheeks with characteristic tenderness.

Like Gabe himself, within the first few minutes of meeting her, he'd been won over by Andrea. She had a warmth and vibrancy that engulfed you, much like Gabe's grandmother who'd passed on. Already Gabe could see Andrea would be the life-giving elixir his grandfather needed.

"Come in the house—" He motioned to Fabrice. "We'll drink a toast to Gabriel's return."

Fabrice patted his arm. "I'd like to stay, but I have to get back to work. Don't worry. I'll be coming around a lot from now on."

"You make sure you do," Jacques warned him.

Gabe walked his friend to the car. "I'll call you day after tomorrow, Fabrice. We'll make arrangements to go out on the boat alone and catch up."

As he reached in his pocket for his wallet, a dark expression crossed over Fabrice's face. "You insult me by wanting to pay. Don't you know I've been waiting years for this day to come?"

"So have I," Gabe whispered.

"Then why did you stay away so long?"

The two men eyed each other solemnly. "The next time we get together alone, I'll tell you."

"You swear?" Fabrice demanded. Emotion caused the veins to stand out in his neck.

"I swear, *mon ami.*"

"I'm holding you to that." He punched him playfully in the shoulder before getting in his car. After he started the engine he said, "Did anyone know you were coming?"

"No."

There was a slight pause. "Do you want it to stay that way?"

"If I did, it's too late now. My cousin Rene saw me while we were getting our luggage."

Fabrice smacked his forehead. "That's right— He works for the airline now."

"Evidently," Gabe murmured. "After doing a double-take, he picked up the phone. No doubt he called Tante Cecile. By now I would imagine the whole family knows I'm back."

"You mean he didn't rush over to you? Not even to say hello?" his friend asked incredulously. His righteous indignation was a balm to Gabe's soul.

"No."

Cecile had been the cruelest to Gabe's mother during the early years. Unfortunately her husband and children had been infected with her bias.

His aunt Helene had been cold in the beginning too, but by the time of the divorce, she'd learned to tolerate his mother though her husband and children still remained aloof.

"*Mon Dieu*—what happened to cause a breach that has lasted this long?"

"Like I said, the next time we're alone…"

After he drove off, Gabe took the steps two at a time and entered the house. Fabrice had brought all the suitcases inside and had left them in the foyer. Gabe found his grandfather showing Andrea the family photographs placed around the living room.

She was getting a history lesson right off whether she wanted one or not. But Andrea listened attentively to everything his grandfather said. In fact she'd started asking questions she hadn't posed to Gabe. The two of them were so engrossed, he suspected they didn't know he'd come in the room.

When the phone rang, Gabe was closest to the study. He stepped across the hall to answer it.

"Allo?"

The person on the other end didn't say anything. Before long he heard a click. One down, a dozen more to go.

It rang again. He picked up. *"Gabriel Corbin ici."*

"So it's true. You really came!"

He recognized her voice at once. She was his father's older sister. *"Oui,* Tante Helene."

"Cecile called me a few minutes ago to tell me Rene had seen you at the airport terminal. I assumed you would head straight to Jacques's house. You always did favor him."

Gabe blinked. He heard hurt in her voice just now which surprised him.

"It's only natural since he and Marguerite never took sides against your mother. I'm sorry that I did. I was a fool." Her admission amazed him. "Rene said you were with a beautiful blond woman."

"Yes. Her name is Andrea. She's my wife."

"You're married?" she cried. "Does your father know?"

"Not yet."

"But this is unbelievable. How long will you be here before you leave again?"

"I'm here to stay."

"I don't understand."

"Then I'll explain it to you. I've come home for good."

"You must be making a joke. How can you run your affairs from here?"

"Because I sold the company and have decided to earn my daily bread here like the rest of my family."

"A man with your wealth doesn't have to make a living," she scoffed.

"Since I gave all the money I made to charity, I'm afraid I do."

A long silence ensued. "Do you swear you're telling me the truth?"

"I swear," he said for the second time in the last ten minutes.

"Gabriel—what has happened to you?" she cried, sounding genuinely concerned.

"I met the right woman. It put things into perspective for me."

"This is the most incredible news. Your brothers are going to be overawed that their famous brother is back for good. They secretly idolize you, you know."

"I'm a stranger to them, Tante Helene."

"No, Gabriel. You have been the constant topic of conversation in this family since the day you left. We are all very proud of your success."

"All?" he mocked.

"Yes, though there are certain people who will never tell you that to your face."

"Even my father?"

"Especially your father. He has kept every magazine and news article about you. When the family gets together, he shows them to everyone and brags about his son who has the brains of a genius. I have seen tears in his eyes many times, even when he's sober, which isn't very often these days."

Her last comment stunned him.

"It's good you've come home. Your family needs you. Your father needs you."

"He has never needed me."

"That's not true, Gabriel. It's just that you're different from your brothers. Giles wanted to be all things to you, but sensed he could lose you, especially after your mother left. When you went away, he started drinking too much. He still drinks too much."

This was the first Gabe had heard of it. His grandfather had never let on, but then he wouldn't. He hadn't wanted Gabe to feel any worse than he already did about a situation that could never be rectified.

"I've said too much, haven't I."

"Don't worry about it, Tante Helene. You're the one person in the family who has never been afraid to tell the truth as you see it. I must admit I've always admired that trait in you, even when it hurt. I'm glad to learn some things haven't changed."

"I'm glad you're home at last, Gabriel. I've been as worried over Papa as I've been about my brother. With you back, things have to get better."

His father's drinking problem was the real reason Jacques had lost weight?

"Welcome home. Tomorrow night you and your wife must come to our house for dinner. I'll invite everyone and we'll celebrate. It's time the whole family put aside their differences and met under the same roof again. It's the way it should be."

Except for Gabe's mother who wouldn't be there.

"Much as I appreciate it, you'd better hold off until I've had a chance to visit with Papa."

"Tonight would be a good time to do that. He'll probably be at the Petit Marin."

The Little Sailor was the oldest local bar on the island.

"How do you know I'll find him there?"

"Because for years that's where he has gone most nights after fishing."

Gabe felt like someone had just planted a fist in his gut.

CHAPTER FIVE

ANDREA felt rather than heard Gabe enter the upstairs bedroom Jacques had designated for their use.

She'd been standing at the window looking out at the calm sea, waiting for her husband to get off the phone. Her dread of what the call might have done to him prevented her from lifting a finger to unpack.

Sensing his presence, she wheeled around. One look at his distinct pallor and her worst fears were realized. The carefree man laughing with Fabrice on the way home from the airport was nowhere in evidence.

"You look like you're carrying the burden of the world on your shoulders. What else is wrong besides the obvious?" she cried softly.

He stood at the end of the double bed with his hands formed into fists at his side. "Tante Helene phoned. She told me something my own grandfather has chosen to keep from me all these years."

Andrea moved closer. She couldn't bear to see the anguish in his eyes. "What is it?"

"Since I left, it seems my father, who was always temperate in his habits, is drinking very heavily."

As distressing as that news was, Andrea couldn't honestly say she was surprised. A good man who'd prevented his own flesh and blood from returning home, had to deal with the pain and guilt somehow.

Yet she was convinced Gabe's father had to possess

some remarkable virtues, otherwise he wouldn't have raised a son as outstanding as Gabe.

In a way, hearing this news made Gabe's father more human, but it didn't erase the fact that he had a terrible addiction. One that was difficult for most people to overcome. But not impossible.

"No wonder Jacques has been depressed. Under the circumstances it's providential you've come home."

Gabe's jaw hardened before he grasped her shoulders. "I should never have dragged you into this *cauchemar*."

She didn't need a translation to understand he meant nightmare. But what was he saying to her now? That since learning the truth about his father, he regretted his impulsive decision to get married and try for a baby?

If Gabe thought the situation was more than she could handle, and he intended to put her on the next plane out of here, he could think again.

She lifted her proud chin. "You gave me a choice, remember? In fact you painted such a grim picture of what I would face if I married you, I dare say any other woman would have run from you and never looked back.

"But I'm not any other woman. I'm *me*." Her voice throbbed. "So unless you feel the relationship between us isn't working out after all, I'm here to stay until it becomes clear we don't have a future together."

His fingers tightened on her flesh through her cotton top. "*Mon Dieu*, Andrea, you're the one thing that *is* working out." Already he was reverting to type as more and more French kept slipping into his conversation without him being aware of it.

"Then don't shut me out. Let me help you," she implored. "You were right about Jacques. He's overjoyed you're home, and he has made me feel welcome."

"Thank goodness for that," he muttered before wrapping her in his arms. They felt like steel bands, crushing her tighter and tighter. This wasn't the embrace of a lover. He needed someone outside his family circle he could trust and confide in.

If this was all he ever required of her then so be it, because he was her raison d'être. She loved him enough to do anything for him.

"Your grandfather's fixing dinner for us. I think I should go help him."

"I'm sure he'll appreciate it," he said into her hair. "While you do that, I'm going to take a ride on his bike. I'll be back in time to eat." He gave her a swift kiss on the mouth before leaving the bedroom on the run.

She rushed into the hall after him. He negotiated the stairs of the comfortably furnished house with the speed and grace of an athlete. In the jeans and oyster colored pullover he'd worn on the plane, his hard-muscled physique made him an exciting masculine figure.

Her pulse raced. No man in St. Pierre or anywhere else in the world could compare.

The kitchen and back porch connected by a glass door sat at the rear of the house. While Jacques stirred something in a saucepan on the stove, she saw Gabe disappear out the back with a bike that had seen better days.

She hurried over to the window above the sink. Her hungry gaze followed his progress down the road until she couldn't see him anymore. No telling his destination, her heart lamented. With the salty ocean air filling his lungs, wherever he went it would be a trip down memory lane.

Naturally his nerves clamored for release. What better way to deal with the pain his aunt's phone call had brought him than by exerting himself physically.

She felt a gentle hand on her shoulder. "You love my grandson for himself. That is a blessing I hadn't anticipated."

Andrea knew what he was saying. A billionaire had to worry about such things. She turned to Gabe's grandfather. The old man knew her husband's secrets from the past. There was no need for pretense between them.

"He's my very life, Jacques, but don't be deceived. Gabe didn't marry me for the same reason."

He removed his hand and shook a weathered index finger at her. "Gabriel married you." Obviously in Jacques's mind, that was enough.

"Yes," she whispered. "He did it to help me try to have a baby."

His brown eyes lit up in amusement. "Of course. That's part of the reason a man and woman marry."

"True, but in my case he had another agenda. If I'm not pregnant within six months, I'll have to have an operation that will make it impossible for me to conceive. It's his way of doing penance for not marrying Jeanne-Marie years ago."

His gaze searched hers for several seconds. "He told you about the baby?"

She nodded. "I know it wasn't Yves's."

The old man's eyelids lowered as if some heavy weight were pressing them down. "I'm not so sure about that anymore."

If a lightning bolt had just traveled through her body, she couldn't have been more shocked. Her heart began to thud. "Why do you say that?" she cried.

"*Un moment,*" he said, turning to the stove. "It's time to add the most important ingredient."

Though she was dying inside, she had no choice but to be patient while he poured some wine into the mixture.

"Whatever you're cooking, it smells delicious."

"It's my wife's recipe. We call it bouillabaisse Breton style. If you want to put the bread on the table, I'll find the bowls and the glasses."

The fat golden loaf, or *boule* as Gabe called it, sat on a hand-painted wood cutting board. She placed it on the round table in the corner of the kitchen. It was already covered by a white cloth embroidered above the hem in red, yellow and blue wildflowers.

"This needlework is exquisite. Did your wife do it?"

"*Oui,* and all the curtains in the house."

"Your home is lovely."

"She made it that way."

"I would give anything to have met her. When Gabe and I were in Paris, he took me to a place where they served moules because he said they tasted like your wife's."

He nodded. "My grandsons were—what is the word in English when they can't stop eating?"

"Pigs?" she supplied.

"Ah, *oui*. Peegs."

Even though she was waiting for an explanation of the bombshell he'd dropped a few minutes earlier, she couldn't help but laugh. "According to Gabe, he was the biggest one."

"He was always the best at everything, and the best looking."

Andrea had the impression Jacques's remark was meant to cover more territory than the obvious. She was reminded of Fabrice's comment that his wife always preferred Gabe to him.

"Jacques? Please tell me why you said what you did a minute ago."

At first she thought he hadn't heard her because he moved the saucepan off the burner. But then he turned to her and indicated she should sit down at the table opposite him.

He'd brought the wine bottle with him and poured both of them half a glass. After drinking some, he tapped his heart with his fist.

"Something about that situation never felt right in here. Since the day Jeanne-Marie married Yves, she hasn't been able to look me in the eye. My wife was the first to suspect all may not have been as it seemed."

Andrea was aghast. "Did you tell Gabe's father?"

"We tried, but he refused to listen to anything that might cast a shadow on Jeanne-Marie's character." He exhaled a deep sigh. "There was a good reason for that. You see—when our Giles was in his twenties, it was understood he would marry Evangeline Duprex, Jeanne-Marie's mother.''

What? ''You mean both women—''

''*Oui.* Both women have had a fatal attraction for my son and grandson. Jeanne-Marie wanted Gabriel, Evangeline wanted Giles. But fate stepped in when he was stranded at the Halifax airport with another passenger who happened to be a beautiful and exciting American woman like yourself.

''Giles was attacked by the *coup de foudre.* He brought Carol home to meet the family. Their marriage cut Evangeline's heart to the quick. As a result there has always been grief between our two families. You see, Evangeline and Cecile were best friends from childhood and still are.''

A moan slipped out of Andrea's lips.

''Though it happened a long time ago, I fear that when Jeanne-Marie discovered she was pregnant and told Giles that Gabe was the father, my son didn't dare inquire too deeply into the situation, not after he'd disappointed her mother.''

Andrea took a shuddering breath. ''I can understand that he didn't want to hurt Evangeline again through her daughter, but this was Gabe's whole life on the line!''

''*C'est ça.*'' The old man nodded sadly. ''Whether the baby was Gabe's or Yves's, I would like to think my son told Gabe to stay away because inside he didn't want him to do the honorable thing and marry her. He knew Gabe wasn't in love Jeanne-Marie.

''If I know my Giles, he couldn't condone his son being caught in a loveless marriage. That's what would have happened to Giles if he'd married Evangeline.''

Her eyes closed tightly. The situation was more complicated than she'd ever dreamed. Hearing Jacques talk, Andrea could feel the love he had for both men.

Nothing was ever black or white. When you dug deep enough, the colors became mixed. Somewhere in that mix lay the truth...

''If you're right about this, then Gabe isn't the only one who has been living in a private hell all these years.''

''When Carol divorced him, Giles was a broken man. Then Gabe left. No one has been happy since,'' Jacques muttered.

''How could they be?'' she cried. ''I'm not surprised your son has a drinking problem.''

Jacques frowned. ''You know about that?''

She nodded. ''Your daughter Helene told Gabe on the phone a little while ago. I'm sure that's why he left in such a hurry. There's so much pain and guilt everyone is carrying around, it's going to destroy your family. It has to stop!''

He reached across the table to pat her arm in a consoling gesture.

''Jacques? Did Gabe's mother fall out of love with Giles?''

''No. Otherwise she would taken the children with her. Carol comes every month like clockwork—sometimes twice a month—to visit the boys and her grandchildren. I see the way she looks at Giles, and the way he looks at her...

''Neither of them has ever remarried even though

Evangeline became a widow ten years ago and did everything in her power to kindle Giles's interest.''

"Then why are they divorced?"

"That is another subject my son won't discuss with me, but it should never have happened."

Was Evangeline at the core of their eventual breakup? In a community this connected, it was possible that in the beginning, her jealousy had provoked her into making Gabe's mother feel uncomfortable and unwanted. If that had opened a fissure that grew wider with time, Andrea could understand if Gabe's mother couldn't take any more.

Andrea remembered a certain warning Gabe had given her in Paris. It could apply equally to his mother where Evangeline was concerned.

Few outsiders can make it in such an insular society of people who tend to stick to their own and draw their livelihood from the sea. The rest of my family will crucify you by their unwillingness to get to know you. They might never accept you. I'm telling you all this so there won't be any surprises in case you decide to marry me.

The sound of a door closing and another opening brought Andrea's head around in time to see Gabe enter the kitchen. His all-encompassing gaze indicted them on the spot.

"What's wrong? From the looks on your faces, something serious must have happened while I was out. What is it?" he demanded.

Help!

"Your wife has been telling me about her fear that she won't be able to give you a baby."

Thank you, Jacques.

She felt Gabe's eyes scrutinize her. "The time to worry about that is months away yet."

Andrea swallowed hard. "I know."

Jacques rose to his feet. "Wash your hands, *mon gars,* and we'll eat."

While Gabe did his bidding, Jacques poured the fish soup into their bowls. Twenty minutes later they'd finished off the delicious meal with fruit and cheese. However Andrea would have enjoyed their dinner more if there'd been no underlying tension at the table.

Though Gabe and his grandfather talked fishing, she could tell her husband hadn't been satisfied with Jacques's explanation after walking in the kitchen from his bike ride. Andrea didn't doubt he would grill her when they were alone.

She had no intention of hiding anything from him. On the contrary, she was eager to share what she'd learned. But she didn't feel that their first meal with his grandfather was the time to reopen old wounds that had never healed.

"I saw the new fish processing plant while I was out on your bike."

Jacques nodded while he munched on the last slice of apple. "It's that outfit from Brest with state of the art freezing capabilities. They didn't open it any too soon. Three hundred plant jobs have made a difference for those affected by the moratorium on salmon fishing beyond the twelve-mile boundary."

Because of what Gabe had confided to her, Andrea knew St. Pierre had been going through severe economic difficulties. What country wasn't? But without Gabe's help, theirs would be particularly hard hit when their sole resource for revenue was the sea. "When were they told they couldn't fish for salmon where they wanted?"

"A law was passed in 1999," Gabe informed her. "It affected fishing for the blue-fin tuna as well. There are programs underway to rebuild the stock, but these things take time."

Jacques nodded. "Bertrand and Philippe have become distributors for the new company. The pay is excellent."

"Good for them." A strange smile broke out on Gabe's face just then, one Andrea recognized after having worked with him for six months. He was secretly pleased his efforts to help his family were working...

"Their wives wouldn't agree with you. They don't like my grandsons to travel."

Andrea could relate. Now that she was married to Gabe, the thought of him leaving the island for weeks at a time would be anathema to her. But if a man needed work... "Where do they have to travel, Jacques?"

His dark eyes flicked to hers. "Wherever they can open up new markets. Canada and the East Coast of the U.S. are saturated, so they've concentrated on U.S. customers further inland."

"What kind of products do they sell exactly?"

"Cod fillets, flounder, sole, ocean perch, chowder fish."

"Um. I love perch. It has a sweet, mild flavor. I'm sure Gabe's brothers won't have any problem if they sell exclusively to small restaurant owners and avoided a middle man," she theorized.

"People who don't live near an ocean crave sea-food. When you travel through the Great Plains for instance, most menus only offer nasty fried shrimp coated in too much breading. It tastes of the carton because it has probably been sitting at the bottom of some freezer for years."

Both men burst into laughter.

Gabe's eyes gleamed unexpectedly before he reached for her hand and squeezed it. "My wife the entrepreneur. Now you know why I made her my chief software engineer, Grand-père."

"Better not let her near that plant or she'll get so busy revolutionizing everything, you'll never see her," Jacques teased.

"There's no chance of that," Gabe said, still caressing her fingers. "We have another project that's going to take up a lot of our time."

His comment piqued his grandfather's interest. "What is that, *mon gars?*"

"We've bought a house. Now we have to restore it."

"I see." Jacques's expression looked pained. Andrea could understand. They'd barely arrived on the island, and already he thought Gabe was talking about moving. "Where?"

"Considering it's on St. Pierre, it isn't too far from you."

The old man was in so much distress he had to clear his throat several times. No doubt he'd been hoping Gabe would live with him.

Andrea pressed her husband's fingers as her way of begging him not to keep his grandfather in suspense any longer. Their gazes locked before he let go of her hand and gave Jacques his full attention.

"It must be over on the other side by the new plant," his grandfather said beneath his breath but she heard him.

"Why do you presume that?"

"Because no one on this side gives up their house to anyone but another family member."

Gabe leaned toward Jacques. "Sometimes they make an exception if it's the grandson of the family member's best friend."

Jacques seemed to stagger in the chair. He stared at Gabe for the longest time. "*You* bought Gorky's house?"

"Yes and I told the realtor his life wouldn't be worth *un sou* if he didn't warn Gorky's wife to keep it a secret from you until after I got here."

Tears sprang into Jacques's eyes. Andrea could see his heart was too full to talk. He lifted his hands to Gabe's cheeks, the way he'd undoubtedly done to him when he was a little boy. For the next few minutes he simply held on to him.

It was one of those sweet moments that would stay in Andrea's memory for as long as she lived.

"After the dishes are done, how would you like to come with me and Andrea in our new car? I want to show her the island before the sun goes down."

"What new car?" she blurted.

Gabe turned to her. If she didn't miss her guess, his beautiful gray eyes exhibited a wet sheen put there by strong emotion.

"The one out in front. I ordered it last week and

told them to have it ready when we arrived this afternoon.''

''So *that's* where you went on the bike.'' She'd known he'd ridden off in pain, yet somehow the knowledge that he'd had a specific reason to leave made her feel a little better.

Jacques was first up from the table. He looked excited. ''You two go on and enjoy yourselves before you can't see anything. I'll clean up the kitchen, then I'm going to have a tête-à-tête with Karmele.''

Andrea cleared the table before running upstairs to comb her hair and put on fresh lipstick. The temperature at the airport had been in the mid-seventies. It probably wouldn't drop lower until dark, so she didn't bother to take a wrap.

Still dressed in the same lime-green cotton pants and white top she'd worn on the plane, she hurried down the stairs and out the front door to join Gabe. He helped her into their new blue four-door family car.

Her husband could have bought anything, but again he showed restraint in his choice. The flashy sports car he used to drive cost more than most islanders' annual income and would be totally out of place here.

Once he was behind the wheel and they'd taken off she couldn't resist saying, ''You've made a new man of your grandfather. It's too bad you didn't decide to come back to St. Pierre while your grandmother was still alive.''

He flashed his eyes at her with an intense regard. ''If I'd done that, I wouldn't have met you.''

Her breath caught. ''Gabe—you don't need to pretend with me when we're alone like this.''

"Who's pretending?" he fired back.

"You are. Your grandfather thinks ours is a love match. We both know differently."

His hands gripped the steering wheel tighter. "As I told you in Paris, we have mutual trust and admiration for each other. There isn't another woman I would have wanted to bring home with me. And the more I'm around you, the more I know you'll be a wonderful mother to our child."

She lowered her head. "If we have one." Her voice wobbled.

"There's no 'if' about it!"

His nerves appeared as ragged as hers.

"What else were you and Grand-père talking about before I came in earlier?"

Andrea had been waiting for him to ask that question.

She realized Jacques wouldn't have shared so much private information with her if he hadn't wanted her to be in possession of all his suspicions. In fact he'd probably told her everything in the hope that she would talk to Gabe about them. Now was her opportunity.

"Both your grandparents believed Jeanne-Marie might have lied when she told your father she was pregnant with your baby."

The second the words left her lips Gabe braked so forcefully, the car rocked in place next to the stone wall separating the road from the calm water. Thankfully no cars had passed them along this section yet.

Her body tautened. Though the deepening twilight had stolen over the peaceable surroundings punctuated by the sound of a distant buoy, there was a storm raging inside her husband. He raked a hand through his black wavy hair.

"How long has he had these suspicions?" His voice sounded like it had come from an underground cavern.

His question was the first one Andrea had wanted the answer to after Jacques had taken her into his confidence. Without pausing for breath, she told Gabe everything. When she'd finished, it was getting too dark for her to see his expression clearly.

"Do you mean to tell me Grand-père believes my father told me to stay away out of fear I'd feel obliged to marry Jeanne-Marie?"

"Yes. Jacques told me the history between Evangeline and your father. When he married your mom instead of her, it caused trouble. After what your father went through, I can understand why he might have worried you would feel pressured to tie yourself to a woman you didn't love. It makes sense that he wanted to help him the only way he knew how."

She heard a lethal curse come out of Gabe before he said, "I don't know what the truth is, but I'm sure as hell going to find out!"

Like lightning he made a U-turn, causing her head to swim. They sped back to the house. "Forgive me, Andrea, but the tour of the town will have to wait."

"I understand," she whispered. "There's a lot of unpacking I have to do." She reached for the door handle.

"I'll probably be home late. Don't wait up for me."

"I won't."

With her heart breaking, she got out of the car and

hurried up the steps. Before she had time to close the front door of the house, she heard the tires screech as Gabe quickly drove away. He'd made another U-turn and was headed for the city center.

The premonition she'd had on the plane had come true. Tonight wouldn't be like the other rapture filled nights she'd spent with him at her parents' home in Scarsdale.

Luckily Jacques was still visiting his neighbor and couldn't see her glistening face as she dashed up to the guest bedroom.

The Petit Marin had always catered to an older crowd. The wooden sign, a depiction of a little child in a sailor's suit sitting on a dock swinging his legs, still hung over the eaves above the doorway.

Gabe walked inside. Nothing about the place had changed in all these years. His gaze swept the dimly lit room searching for his father who was wiry and resembled a younger Jacques to a great degree. Both possessed black hair, brown eyes and were five-eleven, the same height as the twins, though his grandfather had shrunken a little.

Over the years Jacques had sent pictures so Gabe could keep up with the changes to his family as everyone matured. The most recent photos of his father revealed a man with gray at the temples and a considerable paunch, something Gabe never expected to see.

He'd assumed his parent had put on excess weight from overeating. Now he knew differently.

The barman who'd been scrutinizing Gabe in an effort to place him because he looked familiar, greeted him. "What would you like to drink?"

"I'm looking for Giles Corbin, but I don't see him."

There was a slight pause on the other man's part before he murmured, "It is strange. He's usually here at this time, but not tonight."

"Merci." He placed twenty francs on the bar and left the premises before the man who'd put two and two together could start asking a lot of questions Gabe had no intention of answering.

By now word would have reached his father Gabe had returned. The shock would have set him back. It was possible he'd retreated to another bar.

Then again he might have gone to his fishing boat to drink himself into oblivion using something stronger than wine without anyone else being witness. Gabe should have thought to look for him there first.

He got in his car and drove to another section of the island where the bigger boats and fishing trawlers were moored. It was night. All the vessels were in, including his father's located midway down the pier.

Gabe parked his car and got out. After negotiating the cement steps, he walked the planks toward the *Alouette.*

Most of the men had gone home by now, but there were still a few doing last minute chores to get ready for the next morning's run. He could hear their voices in passing.

The sight of the *Alouette* brought back a flood of memories, but the boat should have been replaced years ago. It looked deserted, but that didn't necessarily mean his father wasn't here.

He climbed on board and descended the stairs to the living quarters where he expected to find him slumped over the table with an empty bottle of vodka lying on the floor. Except for the creaks and lapping of water against the hull, all was quiet.

"Papa?" he called out. An inspection of the sleeping area produced no results, either.

Gabe didn't want to confront him at the house. Since times had grown lean, Philippe and his family had moved in with their father. Maybe his alcoholism was another reason Gabe's younger brother had made that decision.

In any case, Celeste would be putting their children to bed. A reunion under such strained circumstances would make it uncomfortable for everyone.

Better to come back here at dawn and catch his father alone. He'd always been known as an early riser. However that may have changed if he had a long history of being hung-over.

Defeated for the moment, Gabe retraced his steps to the car and drove back to his grandfather's. If things were different, he might have been tempted to pay another visit to the Petit Marin and dull his senses with drink.

But he had Andrea waiting for him, thank God. He needed her arms around him tonight, her avid mouth on his.

Her desperation to have a baby made her the kind of lover most men could only dream about. He never had to worry she didn't want him. It didn't matter what time of night or morning, she was always ready for him, giving him kiss for kiss, overwhelming him with passion.

He was terrified that when the six months were up

and she was either pregnant or forced to have the operation, everything was going to change.

No matter how much pain he'd suffered in his life, Gabe knew it would be nothing compared to the pain he would have to endure if the ecstasy she gave him had all been manufactured in order for her to conceive. Somehow he had to find a way to make her fall in love with him.

So far he'd gone about everything wrong. As much as he needed to talk to his father after all these years and see if they could achieve some kind of pax, Andrea was the one who needed him tonight.

He'd brought her to a strange country, away from work and family, from everything familiar. Then he'd promptly left her while he went out hunting for the man who'd told him never to come home again.

Though he could see she and his grandfather were already getting along famously, Gabe had thrown her in at the deep end and expected her to swim alone in strange waters. What kind of a monster was he?

After being away so many years, he wasn't going to be able to put his world back together overnight. Andrea was a different matter. She was his wife!

If he didn't do everything possible to help her adjust to this new way of life, he might lose her long before the six months were up.

He couldn't let that happen. There was no way he'd let it happen.

When his grandfather's house came into view, he parked the car off the road and raced inside to find her.

CHAPTER SIX

AFTER unpacking all their cases, Andrea had gotten ready for bed and had just slid under the covers when she heard the bedroom door open.

She saw her husband's tall, powerful physique silhouetted by the faint light from the stairway down the hall.

After knowing he'd gone to see his father, she hadn't expected him back for hours. In fact if the two men were able to communicate, it wouldn't have surprised her if he didn't come home until the next day. Too many years had gone by. There was a lifetime to catch up on.

Something must have gone wrong.

"Gabe?" she called out in alarm, sitting up against the headboard.

"Stay where you are, *mon amour.*" He shut the door. "I'll join you in a minute."

The endearment came as a total surprise. On their wedding night she'd asked him not to call her darling. But Gabe wasn't one to be thwarted and had reverted to French to get around her. Right now he didn't sound or act like the same demon-driven man who had left her behind earlier.

His behavior then had been so unlike the man she'd fallen in love with, it had given her a further glimpse into his tortured emotions. She'd been haunted by it all evening.

Letting out a troubled sigh, Andrea lay back down and waited for him to shower, not knowing what to think. When she tried to put herself in his place, she couldn't.

She remained in an anxious state until she felt his side of the bed give. In the next instant he reached for her with an urgency that sent liquid fire through her body. Somehow she'd thought he would want to talk, but that came much later after he'd made love to her with almost refined savagery.

"Forgive me for being so abrupt with you earlier tonight," he whispered against the side of her neck as he rocked her in arms.

"There's nothing to forgive. You'd just heard news that tore you apart. You think I don't know that?"

"It was no excuse for my rudeness to you."

"You didn't do anything wrong, Gabe. You were in pain."

"I swear I'll never let it happen again. You're the one person I never want to hurt."

Where was all this coming from? "You didn't hurt me," she assured him. "Tell me what happened tonight."

His arm tightened around her. "I looked for my father in the two places I felt he might be. But I should have anticipated he'd probably stayed home where he knew I wouldn't have the temerity to show my face."

Andrea rubbed the back of his neck with her hand. "Perhaps he was hoping it was the first place you would come."

"I don't think so. Our business is for our ears alone. My brother and his family live with Papa."

"How do you know he didn't ask them to spend

the night somewhere else, hoping against hope you would show up?''

''I can't imagine him doing that.''

''Don't dismiss the possibility. Has it occurred to you he might be in pain because you chose to stay with Jacques instead of coming to see him first?''

His hand tightened in her hair. ''You've taken my grandfather's side.''

''We're both on yours—'' she cried gently. ''You have to know that!''

At her answer, she felt his hard body let go of some of the tension. ''There's a saying I once heard. I wonder if it could apply to your father, Gabe.''

He pressed a thorough kiss to her lips. ''What is it?''

''Something like, I can't find peace, but I'm afraid to wage war.''

He heaved a heavy sigh and rolled on his back. ''So you're suggesting I should have gone straight to his house from the airport and forced him to face his fear.''

She leaned over him. ''No—I wouldn't presume to tell you anything. I'm only thinking out loud.''

He traced the line of her mouth with his index finger. ''Whether you meant to or not, you've made me decide something.''

Her heart skipped a beat. ''What is it?''

''I was planning to go to his fishing boat before sunup and wait for him to arrive. But there'll be other fishermen out there already. They're all friends of my father's. Word travels faster than the Internet around here, which means the island knows I'm back.

''Before he or my brothers have even seen me, it

wouldn't be fair for them to hear from everybody else first that I'm on the boat. After all this time, the last thing I want to do is put them in an awkward position in front of their friends.

"So, *mon coeur,* you and I will spend the day together tomorrow. At dinnertime, we'll drop by my father's house for a visit like any normal newlyweds anxious to see their family. Whatever will be, will be."

A small gasp escaped her throat. "Don't you want to go alone for your first visit?"

"No. I've discovered I need my wife, and I want you with me every step of the way."

Andrea realized that facing his father like that was going to be the hardest thing he'd ever done Though she knew Gabe wasn't in love with her, it thrilled her that he wanted her support. After speaking her thoughts, she feared she might have alienated him.

He reached for her hand and kissed the palm. "Before we begin our sightseeing in the morning, we'll run by the hospital and make an appointment with the best gynecologist they recommend."

"There's nothing wrong with me at the moment."

"That's right, and I want things to stay that way. Once you *are* pregnant, it'll be better if you've already established a rapport with your doctor, don't you agree?"

"Yes, of course. Thank you for thinking of that. To be honest, I—"

"You've been forced to concentrate on my problems," he broke in. "It's time we focused on you and the baby we're going to have. If I know Grand-père, he has arranged for us to take a look at Karmele's house. Once we get inside, we can determine where we'd like to put a nursery.''

Gabe's thoughts were never far removed from the child he hoped was on the way this month. She had the feeling he was going to be as crushed as she would be if her period came. It was due in ten days or less.

According to the result of her fertility kit test, plus her temperature which had spiked the day before yesterday, she'd ovulated in the last few days. But that didn't necessarily mean conception had occurred. So many factors played into it. The very fact that they were trying this hard could be the one thing that prevented it from happening.

''What are you thinking about, *Madame Corbin?*''

She drew in a ragged breath. ''A lot of things.''

''That's fine as long as you don't do it from so far away. Come here,'' he coaxed in a low, sensuous male voice. The second his compelling mouth claimed hers, she found herself caught up in ecstasy only her husband could create. If she could have one wish, it was that this night would last forever...

There was a gentle tap on the bedroom door. *''Mon gars—''*

Gabe rolled away from his wife who was sleeping soundly and lifted his head.

''Gabriel—''

So he hadn't imagined his grandfather calling to him. What time was it?

He glanced at his watch. Quarter to seven in the morning. Jacques was probably going fishing and wanted to let them know, but he could have left a note.

There had to be some other reason for disturbing them.

Taking care not to waken Andrea who had to be exhausted after he'd made love to her most of the night, he slid out of bed and tiptoed to the bathroom for his robe. Once his belt was tied, he left the room as quietly as he could and shut the door behind him.

One look in his grandfather's eyes told him it was serious.

He put a hand on Gabe's arm. "Giles is downstairs. I'm going to the *boulangerie*."

Of all the scenarios he could have imagined, Gabe never expected his father to seek him out here, catching him off guard. Maybe it was the shock of realizing this moment had come that left him feeling strangely numb.

Like a sleepwalker, he followed his grandfather down the hall to the stairs.

The second he spied his parent at the foot, he was thankful Jacques had sent him recent pictures. Otherwise it would have shaken him to see his sixty-year-old father looking ten years older and vaguely debauched.

Comments his mother used to make about him and how attracted she was to his handsome Gallic looks screamed at Gabe now.

Fathoms deep in memories that sliced through him like knives, Gabe wasn't even aware of his grandfather's disappearance. At the moment he saw only two things—fear and pleading coming from his father's dark brown eyes.

"G-Gabriel—" his parent whispered brokenly. "You have every right to despise me forever— But I want you to know that every second, every minute, every hour of every day since I told you not to come home, I have longed for my son.'' His chin literally trembled as the tears poured down his flushed cheeks.

His father had to cling to the banister for support. Pure revelation flowed through Gabe that his father had suffered in more ways than he'd ever dreamed or imagined.

Gabe continued down the stairs toward him.

''I don't deserve anything, *mon fils,* but by some miracle the Blessed Virgin has preserved my life long enough to lay eyes on you again and see for myself what a splendid, magnificent man you've become. Now I can die.''

Hot, searing pain shot through Gabe, melting away the numbness that had held him trapped inside his body for the last few minutes. ''Why would you want to do that?''

''Because I'm your father, and I failed you even though I was convinced I was doing the right thing for you.''

All this time Gabe thought he'd pushed him away to protect Yves. But Andrea had forced him to consider what his grandfather had told her, that his father hadn't wanted him to feel obligated to marry Jeanne-Marie. Was his wife right?

''I believe you.''

His father looked staggered by Gabe's assertion.

''But I hurt you, Gabriel. I caused you pain when it was the last thing I wanted to do—and there's no forgiveness for that. I've missed you—and there's no getting back the years—''

He broke off sobbing. They were wretched sobs that shook Gabe's soul.

"Maybe not those years, Papa. But there are still many yet to come for you and me to enjoy together."

His father's head lifted abruptly. The shocked expression on his anguished face twisted Gabe's emotions even more. "What are you saying?"

"Just this," Gabe began after trying to swallow, but couldn't. "The past is what it is. We can't change it, and now it's behind us where it belongs.

"I've come home for good because this is where my family is. It's where I want to raise my own family."

His father's hand went out, as if he were shielding himself from too bright a sun. "But you couldn't want that now. You're a very important man with enormous responsibilities. There's nothing for you here."

Gabe's heart bled for his broken parent whose inability to forgive himself had turned him into a tragic figure. "Have you stopped loving me, Papa?"

The tears dripped steadily off his father's chin. "I love you too much. That has been the problem."

Those words etched themselves in Gabe's heart. "I never stopped loving you either, *mon père.*"

"Gabriel—"

His cry of disbelief sounded like a moan. Gabe reached out to embrace his father. After so many years apart, it was cathartic to feel him kissing Gabe's cheeks, begging his forgiveness.

"There's nothing to forgive, Papa. I'm the one to blame for staying away so long. Pride prevented me from calling you."

"No—" His father shook his head. "You thought

I didn't love you anymore. You feared that if you got in touch with me, I would reject you.

"On my part I was terrified of the damage I'd done without meaning to. I felt you were better off without me, so I resisted the temptation to call you. But I wanted to! Every day I wanted to. Instead, I called Papa. He was my lifeline to you."

Gabe cleared his throat. "I used Grand-père the same way because I had to know how you were. Now that we both know the truth, I want to be an integral part of this family again. You're going to love Andrea."

"Andrea?"

Just the way his father said her name, Gabe realized his father was in the dark about a lot of things.

"How did you know I'd flown in?"

His father averted his eyes. "I...didn't get home until late last night. When the phone rang it was Papa. He called to tell me you had just arrived at the house."

Bless you, Grand-père.

"Then let me be the first to announce I brought my bride with me. She came to work for me six months ago. During the initial interview, I felt something for her I've never felt for another woman.

"She became my chief software engineer, but that still wasn't enough for me. So I married her ten days ago in New York City."

"Bravo!" He hugged Gabe again and wept a little more. After wiping his eyes he said, "Does your mother know?"

His mother...

Their divorce was another mystery. Especially since

it was clear to Gabe that his father was still very much in love with her.

"Yes. We talked to her on the phone last week while we were staying with Andrea's parents. She's going to fly out to meet her after we're settled in our own home."

"Your own home…" he whispered, then scratched his head. "Are you building a branch of your company here?"

Gabe could see this was going to take time.

"Papa? Let's go in the kitchen for a cup of coffee and I'll explain everything. We've got years to catch up on, and there are important matters I want to discuss with you about the future of the island."

His father's eyes pulsated with new light.

By tacit agreement they filed through to the rear of the house. Jacques had already made coffee. Gabe reached for the rest of the bread they hadn't eaten the night before and put it on the table.

No stranger to the kitchen which had seen three generations of Corbins raised in it, his father found the mugs in the cupboard. Once the steaming brew had been poured, they sat down.

Gabe watched him dunk his brioche into the scalding liquid the way he'd done thousands of times before. That gesture perhaps more than any other brought the past flooding back, yet somehow there wasn't the terrible pain connected with the memory.

It was like déjà vu, but different. Gabe felt a camaraderie with his father that was new. On his part, he no longer felt guilty for being different from his brothers. On his father's part, Gabe didn't seem to intimidate him anymore.

A bonding had taken place at the bottom of the staircase. Their long separation seemed to have accomplished something that the first eighteen years of living with his father hadn't done.

"My wife and I will be moving into Gorky's house as soon as Karmele vacates it," Gabe began.

His father looked too happy and simply shook his head in disbelief.

"We need to get settled right away. Andrea has a medical problem I want to tell you about, and there's the matter of her fitting in around here. You know how hard it was for Maman. Maybe you can advise me what to do to help my wife adjust."

Though he'd discussed Andrea's condition with his mother over the phone in private, it felt good to be confiding in his father as well.

Giles eyed him frankly. "You're asking my advice when you know your mother left me?"

"Yes."

His father groaned. "I failed her too, *mon fils.*"

"How?" Maybe Gabe was finally going to learn why there'd been a divorce.

"Don't ask," he begged.

Andrea awakened to an empty bed. After the passion that had flared between them during the night, Gabe must have assumed she needed her sleep.

The intensity of his lovemaking might have led her to believe he was becoming emotionally involved... Except for the one glaring fact that he'd felt guilty for his dark mood earlier. She suspected he'd tried to make up for it. But morning had brought him to his senses. No doubt he'd been eager to join his grandfather for breakfast. Andrea certainly didn't begrudge them their precious time together.

Gabe's disappearance from their bedroom gave her an opportunity to wash her hair and put on a new outfit to go sightseeing with him. It was a sundress with cap sleeves. She loved the all-over blue and lavender print on white, and had bought white sandals to match.

Before leaving New York she'd had her blond hair cut in a layered bob. The stylist told her the long crown layers, shorter sides and blunt back gave her a sophisticated, classy look. Andrea didn't know about that. The only thing that mattered was the immediate glint of male approval in Gabe's eyes when he first saw her.

It was an easy hairdo to maintain. With her natural curl, all she had to do was dry it with a towel and brush it into place. Some pink frost lipstick, a poof of wildflower splash and she was ready.

Once they started walking around the island, people would recognize Gabe. It was possible they might run into members of his family as well. She wanted him to be proud of her.

Once she'd descended the staircase, she could hear male voices drifting into the foyer. Though she couldn't make out distinct words, it was clear they were enjoying their conversation.

Anxious to start fitting in she said, "*Bonjour,* Jacques," in her best French upon entering the kitchen.

Both men got to their feet. Gabe's silvery-gray eyes swept over her with heart-pounding intimacy, but it wasn't until her gaze transferred from him to his grandfather that she realized her mistake.

It was a younger looking Jacques who stood before her. She'd seen his picture along with the others in the living room.

Too late to prevent it, a small gasp escaped her lips.

"*Mon amour,* this is my father, Giles Corbin. Papa? Meet Andrea, my other half."

Something miraculous had happened for them to be this congenial, but she would have to practice patience until she was alone with her husband and he could tell her everything.

"Welcome," the older man said and embraced her warmly, kissing her on both cheeks three times in a row. "My son is much more like me than I thought," he declared with unfeigned emotion. "We may be Bretons inside and out, but it seems only a beautiful American woman holds the key to our hearts."

He was wrong, of course. Gabe's heart wasn't involved. But this moment didn't have anything to do with Andrea. It was about a father and son who after years of suffering had found each other again. She wanted to cry for joy.

"Thank you," she murmured, studying the lines of suffering in his good-looking face whose bone structure he'd bequeathed to his son. "I've longed to meet you. Gabe's such a remarkable man, I knew he had to have wonderful parents."

While he stared at her assimilating her words, his dark brown eyes flickered in reaction. "We need to get the whole family together tonight for a big celebration, *mon fils.*" His voice sounded thick with feeling. "Everyone must meet Andrea."

Gabe put his arm around her shoulders and pulled her tightly against him. "Tante Helene already phoned here last night suggesting the same thing. I told her it would have to wait until I'd seen you.''

His father nodded. "I'll call her while the two of you are sightseeing. Plan on getting together at seven.''

"Don't leave!" Andrea blurted when she could see he was prepared to walk out of the kitchen. "Gabe and I have months to tour the island together.''

"Years!" her husband amended so forcefully, it shocked her. Yet it shouldn't have. Gabe intended to let the whole world believe they were in love and planned to be together forever.

If Giles felt the sudden tension between her and his son, he didn't let it show.

"Yves will be waiting for me at the boat. As for you, Gabriel has told me about your battle with endometriosis. It is much more important that you carry through with your plan to visit the hospital this morning.

"I've told him about Dr. Marais, a new specialist in female care. Lucie went to see him when she had problems during her last pregnancy. He found the problem right away and cleared it up. You'll be in good hands.''

"That's very reassuring, Monsieur Corbin.''

"Please—call me Giles, or even better, Papa?''

The pleading in his eyes was her undoing. "Papa then.''

"*Merci, ma belle,*" he whispered before kissing her on both cheeks once more.

As he kissed his son with fatherly affection, Gabe's eyes trapped hers. They held a tenderness she'd never seen in them before. Her body quivered in response.

"We'll walk you out, Papa."

When they reached the front porch, Andrea saw that Giles had pulled his car behind their car. Before he reached it, Jacques came pedaling along the road with a couple of baguettes under his arm. He stopped alongside to talk to his son who embraced him fiercely while he was still on his bike.

It was an indescribable feeling to watch a family heal. "I'm so happy for you, Gabe."

The hand around her hip tightened. "We've made a start in the right direction, but I'm less certain than before about what really went on years ago. Fortunately I'm home now and won't rest until I've uncovered every ounce of truth there is."

He sounded in deadly earnest. She turned her head to look at him. "I thought you'd made your peace."

His gaze swerved to hers, but it held an unfathomable expression. "Papa and I have agreed to put the past behind us, but that's all we've done. I asked no questions, he gave no answers."

When Andrea thought about it, she realized Jacques was the person responsible for getting Giles to come to the house. Jacques was also the one who'd voiced his suspicions to her about the baby's paternity so she would tell Gabe. Without the old man's help, Gabe and his father would still be at a stalemate.

She was grateful he'd acted as a catalyst, yet a lot of the happiness she'd been feeling dissipated because Gabe was now armed with new questions to ask. He would be relentless in his search of the facts.

Throughout the rest of the day he played the part of the devoted husband to perfection. They met with Dr. Marais first, then toured the harbor town with its summer street performers and charming boutiques. At the Arche museum no one could have been a more knowledgeable and entertaining guide. She loved every second spent with him.

But behind the facade lurked a man on a mission, one furthermore who she sensed was counting the minutes until they arrived at the family party.

Gabe donned a formal light gray suit for the occasion that brought out the silver of his irises. His grandfather wore navy. Andrea showered before putting on a new sleeveless black silk dress with a mandarin collar her husband had insisted she wear to the party.

He'd bought it for her as a surprise wedding present. The style wasn't her favorite, but when he'd given it to her, he'd told her she would look breathtaking in it. She translated the compliment to mean he wanted her to make a statement when he introduced her to his family for the first time. Was it for Jeanne-Marie's benefit?

When she emerged from the closet wearing it, she thought his eyes flared with passion before his lids lowered. Could he fake that emotion? During that brief, unguarded moment, memories of the night before when his hunger for her had seemed insatiable seemed to heighten her awareness of her handsome husband.

A flush swept over her body before he escorted her out to the car where Jacques was waiting.

At the stroke of seven they pulled up behind a line of cars near his aunt's home on the other side of the island. It was built in a ranch style with a yellow exterior. Gabe got out first to come around and help her. But before he could reach her door, two brown haired men who were Corbins through and through and bore a remarkable resemblance to each other, descended on her husband.

Andrea's heart hammered with tremendous force to watch the brothers' reunion. They were grown men now. The day Gabe had left the island, they'd only been sixteen years old.

Between the shouts of excitement and laughter, she had an impression of faces lit up in pure delight before the hugs and the kisses began.

Beyond the three of them she saw another man descending the porch steps. He appeared older than the others, yet he bore the same striking Corbin family features and stood almost as tall as Gabe.

Even from the distance, Yves's expression had that dark, remote look she'd sometimes seen on Gabe's face when she'd worked for him. He only hesitated for a moment before joining his brothers to welcome the second Corbin son home.

Gabe's grandfather helped Andrea from the car. "While the boys get reacquainted, I'll take you inside and introduce you to everyone else."

"Thank you, Jacques."

He put her arm through his before walking her toward the house. Andrea's gaze flicked to the porch. A brunette woman with expressive dark brows and pouting lips had just come out of the house.

Her eyes focused hungrily on Gabe. They dominated her face which looked devoid of color or animation.

Jeanne-Marie. The girl who'd known Gabe's possession first. The girl now married to Yves, the oldest brother who would be a constant reminder of the man she couldn't have.

Andrea hadn't thought it would bother her to meet the woman from her husband's past. But she was wrong. Dead wrong.

Perspiration broke out on her delicate brow. Her earlier presentiment that more pain lay ahead, perhaps worse than what Gabe had already lived through, had become a reality.

Only this time Andrea was feeling it, too.

CHAPTER SEVEN

JACQUES must have sensed Andrea's trepidation. He drew her closer in a protective gesture as they walked up the steps where the other woman stood as if she were frozen.

"Jeanne-Marie? Meet Andrea, Gabe's wife."

Piercing brown eyes assessed Andrea without a hint of warmth. *"Bonsoir."*

Jeanne-Marie's sullen, one word greeting in French was meant to be off-putting. But after Gabe's warning that the family would close ranks on Andrea, she had expected as much and gathered up her courage.

"Bonsoir, Jeanne-Marie. Enchantée de faire ta connaissance," she answered and extended her hand. Andrea had been practicing the greeting all day. Finally Gabe had declared that her pronunciation was perfect.

The other woman had no choice but to shake her hand. It was a brief, limp gesture to say the least.

Out of the corner of Andrea's eye she saw the approving gleam in Jacques's. It was then she caught sight of Giles who was also wearing a dark blue suit and tie like his father's.

He must have been standing in the entrance the whole time. Judging by the broad smile on his face, he'd witnessed the byplay. He seemed equally pleased with Andrea's response and held out his arms to her. She went into them gladly.

Like an honor guard, the two men escorted her inside the house where she was confronted by the rest of Gabe's family.

If it hadn't been for Jacques and Giles, it would have been a very uncomfortable experience. The children were abnormally quiet. She couldn't say the adults weren't polite, but they weren't forthcoming, either.

If they could be this cold to Andrea, she began to have some idea of how difficult it must have been for Gabe's mother to fit in at the beginning.

Once introductions were made, Helene directed her to the buffet in the dining room and insisted she start first since she was the honored guest. Every eye seemed to be on Andrea as she spooned a little of everything onto her plate.

She was relieved when several of the teens followed her to the living room and sat on the couch at either side of her. They were the high school aged twin son and daughter of Yves and Jeanne-Marie. Andrea sensed their curiosity. She was prepared to indulge them if it would help break the ice.

"I haven't had halibut in years. This is delicious," she said after sampling it.

"It is okay," Robert said with a heavy French accent.

"I suppose when you live by the sea, you can't appreciate how wonderful fresh fish is to someone like me."

Vivienne, the girl on Andrea's other side, turned to her. "What do you eat?" Her French accent was just as pronounced as her brother's, but Andrea was impressed that they all spoke English so well.

"Too much fast food."

At that remark, both teens grinned and started acting more natural.

"When you worked for Gabriel, did you ever fly on his private jet?" Vivienne wanted to know. The rest of the family started to assemble around the room in various chairs and love seats.

"Yes. I've been on it three times." Twice for business, and the last time…for personal business that had resulted in a marriage of convenience. One that would end if she didn't get pregnant.

"How come he didn't bring it to the island?" This from Robert, but she could tell everyone in the room was listening.

"He sold it."

"Why?" The teen's shocked expression was priceless.

"Because he sold his company and has come home where he doesn't need to travel anymore."

"Does he still own his own building in New York?"

"He never owned it, Robert. He leased a couple of floors for his business."

"Does he have homes all over the world?"

"Not that I'm aware of, Vivienne."

"How many bodyguards does he have?"

"None that I know of."

Robert frowned. "But all billionaires have bodyguards!"

Andrea put down her fork. "I think the two of you have the wrong impression of Gabe. His money was tied up in business, not in things. Another company called Karsh Technologies bought him out. Gabe's no longer a billionaire. He's like everyone else around here."

"But if they paid him—"

"He's given the money from his assets to…charity."

A collective gasp resounded in the room.

Vivienne slowly shook her head. "You mean he gave it *all* away?"

"Yes."

The girl's eyes looked at Andrea in stunned disbelief before her gaze fell to her left hand. "Is that why you don't have a huge diamond ring?"

"I suppose so. Gabe surprised me with this gold band."

"Are you upset because he's poor now?"

"No, Vivienne. I'm glad."

"How could you be glad about that?" Robert demanded.

"Because there are a lot more important things in life than the acquisition of money you don't need beyond the necessities. Gabe has ached for his home. He loves the sea."

"Since when?" an older male voice spoke up in a mocking manner. It was Gabe's cousin, Michel, Helene and Auguste's son.

"Since always," she asserted, anxious to defend her husband against the hostility she could feel coming from the adults.

"It may interest you to know Gabe has been a member of the French Fisheries Board for many years. He knows more about what has happened to St. Pierre et Miquelon than anyone else living in this community."

"The French Fisheries Board?" At this juncture she'd caught the attention of Gabe's uncles who stared at her like she'd come from another planet.

"Yes. Without his input over boundary disputes, your islands wouldn't have the protected twelve miles of fishing rights the Canadians planned to take away from you."

On that note Michel stopped eating. So did the others.

Completely worked up at this point, she blurted, hot faced, "The jobs Bertrand and Philippe and hundreds of others have at the new fish processing plant exist because of Gabe!"

"What are you saying?" his aunt Cecile asked the question on everyone's minds. "It's a French company from Brest."

"That's right, created with Gabe's assets and genius."

During Andrea's tour of the island earlier in the day, Gabe had given himself away without meaning to. He knew too much about too many things to do with the island's economy not to be involved at the grassroots level of several moneymaking enterprises.

It was also *his* money backing the new offshore oil drilling ventures that would bring more jobs and hundreds of thousands of dollars to bolster the livelihood of the people. But she kept that to herself. Already she'd given his family too much to assimilate at once.

In fact she was afraid she'd said more than she should have. Gabe wouldn't be pleased. When she heard voices coming from the dining room, she shivered. It meant he and his brothers had entered the house.

Thankful her husband hadn't walked in while she was proclaiming his amazing virtues and accomplishments, Andrea reached for the French bread. Pretending an interest in her food, she took a bite. While she munched, her gaze met Gabe's laserlike glance.

He'd grabbed a ladder-back chair from the dining room and carried it across the expanse where he placed it behind her. Before sitting down, he kissed the back of her neck. "I'm sorry to have fed you to the wolves," he whispered. "I won't leave you alone again."

His brothers brought chairs in, too. Yves entered the living room last with Jeanne-Marie at his side.

There was a pronounced silence while Gabe tucked into his food. Andrea's outburst had given everyone a lot to think about. She hoped the quiet on their end meant they were feeling horrible for having harbored such uncharitable thoughts about him.

Paul, the eleven-year-old son of Philippe, kept staring at Andrea. "How come Oncle Gabriel married you?"

She schooled her features not to reveal how much pain his question had caused her. "We worked together and discovered we liked each other."

"But you're an American!"

"That's true." She smiled. "And you're French. How come?"

"Because I was born here."

"And I was born in New York. Have you ever been there?"

"No, but *mes parents* took me to Montreal."

"I've never been to that city. Did you like it?"

"Yes. It's big."

"So is New York, but I like it here where it's peaceful and the ocean is everywhere you look."

"Wait until there is fog," his mother Celeste spoke for the first time. Her English was precise with only a slight trace of French accent. Andrea had the impression the other woman was trying to make conversation rather than attempting to sour the situation for her.

"Gabe says it can be bad."

Cecile stared pointedly at Andrea. "The winters here are *affreux*."

If Gabe's aunt thought she could upset Andrea with a comment like that, she was very much mistaken.

"They're terrible in New York, too. When the buses and cars can't move because of the snow, and the winds knock out the electricity, all there is to do is bundle up inside the apartment and stay cozy."

Suddenly she felt Gabe's hands on her shoulders from behind. "Why do you think I brought a wife home with me? They turn out to be very useful at times like that."

She blushed from the comment and felt a current of white-hot heat travel through her body at his touch.

By now the men were chuckling. Most of the women smiled. There were two exceptions, Cecile and Jeanne-Marie. Yves's wife sat in the doorway between the dining and living room boldly eyeing Andrea.

Giles must have picked up on Jeanne-Marie's negative feelings. He chose that moment to stand with a wineglass in his hand.

After clearing his throat he said, "I'm thankful to have lived long enough to see the day my second born has come back home to live. Bringing Andrea with him is another great blessing. Welcome, *mes enfants*.''

He saluted the two of them before taking a drink.

By the way Gabe's hands kneaded her upper arms, he was trying to control emotions that had caught him unaware.

''It's wonderful to be back, Papa. I look forward to fishing with you again.'' His voice sounded husky. ''It seems my brothers and cousins are all grown up with wives and children, yet my elders and Grand-père have stayed the same.

''Andrea and I will be living with him until Karmele vacates her house, then we'll move in and make it into our own home. If anyone wants to come and help us paint and repair the roof, we won't turn you away.''

''We'll be there!'' Bertrand and Philippe called out at the same time. Andrea's heart warmed to them for their outpouring of affection for Gabe.

''Thank you for the dinner, Tante Helene. There's nothing like island home-cooking. When Andrea and I are settled, we'll invite everyone over and treat you to some of my wife's German recipes.''

Paul looked at Andrea with a frown. ''I thought you were an American.''

''I am, but my family comes from Heidelberg.''

''They own a nutcracker shop in Scarsdale,'' Gabe supplied.

''A what shop?''

''Funny you should ask.''

An odd inflection in Gabe's voice had Andrea turning her head to see what he was up to. She watched her husband rummage in his suit pocket for the keys to the car. He dangled them in front of Robert.

"If you and Vivienne will open the trunk of my Nissan, you'll find some boxes Andrea's parents shipped here for me. There's a present for everybody."

Gabe—

Andrea hadn't known anything about this.

While the room emptied of all the children who rushed after Robert, she stared at her husband in amazement. In the silence that followed, he pressed a kiss to her astonished mouth.

"Do you think there's anything wrong with my playing *Père Noël* in the middle of June?" he asked against her lips.

"Nothing at all." Those were the only words she could manage to say because she was ready to burst into tears from too much emotion. Gabe had missed out on so many years with his family. She knew there wasn't enough he could do for them.

As the twins came back in carrying two big boxes, it touched Andrea that her husband would have secretly involved her parents and used gifts from their store to help celebrate his homecoming.

For the next ten minutes he was down on his knees, as excited as any child. He found the individual packages and read the names aloud so the children could disperse the right gift to the intended person.

Soon the room grew noisy as each child opened up their box to draw out their own special nutcracker. The older men received smokers while the women marveled over the pyramid/crèche scenes, all made of wood and hand painted in the Black Forest.

"This package is for you," Gabe murmured. His brilliant gaze locked with Andrea's. "We'll put these up at Christmas to remind us of your parents."

Christmas? She didn't imagine she would be here when that holiday rolled around. Yet her pulse raced faster and faster as she opened it and discovered two nutcrackers; The King and Queen of Hearts. Andrea's favorites!

They were a signed pair. Only a few of them existed in the world. For years her parents had displayed them on top of a cabinet, but they were never for sale.

The sheen filming her eyes blurred her vision. "I can't believe Mom and Dad parted with these."

"I had to promise they'd get a grandchild in return," he whispered.

No. That wasn't the reason. Her parents knew the chances of her getting pregnant weren't that great. No... They loved Gabe pure and simple, and could deny him nothing.

She wiped her eyes. "Thank you. These mean more to me than you'll ever know."

The children walked over to Gabe to thank him and kiss his cheeks. She looked around her, thrilled to see that the gifts were a colossal success. Even Cecile and her husband were visibly moved by his thoughtfulness and open generosity.

"Keep the boxes the nutcrackers came in," Andrea advised the children.

"How come?" Paul asked as he kept opening the mouth of his King Richard the lionhearted.

"The value of both grows with time. These will be treasures to hand down to your own children someday."

Before she knew it, she was besieged by Gabe's brothers, including Yves. They thanked her and kissed her warmly. Their wives followed and did the same thing.

Jeanne-Marie performed her part as if nothing was wrong, but she kept her eyes veiled. Andrea knew that for her to have to kiss Gabe's wife in front of him was probably the hardest thing she'd ever been forced to do.

"Sorry we've made such a mess in your living room, Tante Helene."

"Don't apologize, Gabriel. You've delighted everyone." She got up from the love seat to hug him. "Welcome home."

While everyone started to clean up, Andrea slipped into the dining room to clear the rest of the dishes from the table and take them into the kitchen.

Cecile stood at the sink loading the dishwasher. For the moment the two of them were alone. She glanced over her shoulder at Andrea.

"The crèche is very nice. Thank you."

"I'll tell Gabe what you said. The gifts were his idea."

"You're not anything like Gabe's mother."

Andrea blinked. "Is any one person like another?"

"That's what I mean."

"I'm sorry. I don't understand."

"You speak up."

"In other words, she was more timid."

"Yes."

"I understand she was only nineteen when she came to the island. I'm twenty-eight and have been working since college. It makes a big difference."

"Perhaps. Has Gabriel told you about the history between him and Jeanne-Marie?"

Taking a deep breath Andrea said, "Have you always delighted in causing trouble?"

Cecile closed the door on the dishwasher and started it. "I can see that he has. It doesn't bother you?"

"In what way?"

"Knowing your husband was intimate with her? That they made a baby together?"

Andrea wasn't about to discuss Gabe or his brother with her. "I understand there's a question about the paternity of the baby. It might have been someone else's after all."

A sudden gasp came out of Cecile. She put a trembling hand to her throat. "What has Jacques been telling you?"

Why was Gabe's aunt so worried? "He hasn't held back any secrets if that's what you mean."

The older woman shook her head. "H-how did he know about Claude?" she stammered.

Claude—

Good heavens—if Cecile had just said what Andrea thought she'd just said...

"Andrea?"

At the sound of Gabe's voice, his aunt literally trembled. The fear in her eyes confirmed Andrea's suspicions.

She wheeled around to discover her husband's tall, rock-hard physique standing in the doorway. Every time she saw him, she experienced a physical reaction to his presence.

"I've been looking for you, *mon coeur*. Grand-père is tired. I think we should get him home."

"I'm coming." She turned to the older woman who'd gone ashen by now. Her eyes pled with Andrea not to say anything. "*Bonne nuit,* Cecile. I enjoyed our chat."

Gabe wished his aunt good-night, then slid his arm around Andrea's shoulders. "Are you all right?" he asked against the side of her neck before biting her earlobe gently.

"Yes."

Lines darkened his face. "Don't lie to me. Cecile said something to disturb you. Her bite can sting. Those are mother's words."

"In this case I'm afraid she has bitten herself by mistake."

"What happened?" he demanded.

"There's something crucial I have to discuss with you and Jacques, but not until we're alone."

Five minutes later all the thank-yous and good-nights had been said. Gabe gathered up Andrea's nut-crackers and the smoker he'd given Jacques. He couldn't seem to get the three of them out to the car fast enough.

The second he started the engine and they were on their way home, Andrea turned in the seat. Gabe's eyes met hers before she said, "Jacques? Who is Claude?"

The old man's face showed surprise at the unexpected question. "One of Jeanne-Marie's uncles. Why do you ask?"

"Does he live here on the island?"

"No. Evangeline's only brother hated the sea and

didn't get along with their father. He left for France years ago. No one has seen him since.''

"He never married?"

"Not that I've heard."

"When exactly did he leave? Do you remember? It's very important."

Gabe flicked her another searching glance before grasping her hand.

"I remember it well because it was the saddest time in my life," he responded with tears in his voice.

The hand covering Andrea's tightened. "What do you mean, Grand-père?"

"It was the day you left the island, *mon gars*. Your grandmother and I were beside ourselves with pain. So was your father who was still shattered by the divorce. We went over to your house to try to comfort him.

"While we were there, Helene and Cecile came by with more bad news. It seemed Claude had also gone away. Apparently Evangeline was devastated because he was her only sibling."

Andrea's groan coincided with their arrival at the house. Gabe turned off the ignition, but made no move to get out of the car. "What's this all about, Andrea?"

She eyed both men before she said, "I'm sure Evangeline *was* devastated, but it had more to do with the fact that *Claude* was the father of Jeanne-Marie's baby."

In the silence that followed, Jacques crossed himself. Though it was night, Andrea noticed Gabe's arresting features had taken on a chiseled cast.

"Cecile *told* you he molested his own niece?" His

fingers were gripping hers so hard, she realized he didn't know his own strength.

"It slipped out by accident."

"Tell us every word she said," Gabe muttered in a gravelly voice she didn't recognize.

Without preamble Andrea complied. "When you came in the kitchen, she'd just realized her mistake, but it was too late to cover up Evangeline's secret. The terror in her eyes is something I won't forget."

"The question now is, what did Papa know, and when did he know it?"

Gabe's voice was like ice. Andrea shuddered. Her premonition of more pain to come had materialized.

Jacques sat forward and put a hand on Gabe's shoulder. "Go to him tonight and learn the truth once and for all."

"I intend to," he vowed fiercely.

"Y-you don't need to come inside with us, Gabe." Her voice shook. "Jacques and I will be fine."

"Of course we will." He gathered the boxes and got out of the back.

But Gabe came around to her side anyway. He accompanied them up the stairs and opened the front door.

She started to follow his grandfather inside, but Gabe swung her around. "Because of you, I'm going to be able to sort out this nightmare. Thank God for you, Andrea."

He lowered his dark head and gave her a hard, sweet kiss on the mouth that left her whole body trembling.

Long after he'd gotten back in the car and had driven off, she still stood there reeling.

It was the first kiss he'd ever freely given her. But she could never forget he'd done it out of gratitude. All the others kisses had been motivated by his agenda to get her pregnant.

Tears stung her eyes at the bitter irony. Now that he knew Jeanne-Marie's baby wasn't his, the whole situation had changed.

He hadn't lost a child!

He no longer had any reason to go on trying to replace it with another one. The truth was going to change his life.

For the first time since their marriage, Andrea hoped she wasn't pregnant. The chance was slim at best. Now that she was no longer ovulating, it wouldn't be long before her period came.

When that happened it would be the proof she needed to convince Gabe her medical condition was hopeless. He certainly didn't need her to help him deal with his family. The true paternity of Jeanne-Marie's baby had turned everything around.

She could leave Gabe so he'd be free to fall in love with an islander. Someone of his own kind whom his family could embrace, too. A woman without female problems who could give him all the children he wanted when he was ready for them.

"Andrea?" a kind voice called to her. "Are you coming in?"

"Yes. I've just been enjoying the moonlight reflecting on the ocean. It's beautiful." *I'm also thinking it's good Karmele hasn't moved out of her house yet.*

Realizing Jacques was anxious for his son and grandson, she went inside and locked the door after her. He'd climbed halfway up the stairs before she caught up to him. "Are you all right?"

He studied her features. "The truth?"

"Nothing but."

"No one in this family has been all right since Carol left Giles."

Andrea gave him a hug. "Since part of a mystery has been unraveled tonight, maybe there'll be more to unfold. Gabe has come home. Perhaps in time his mother will return for good as well."

He flashed her a brief, sad smile. "That would be too much to hope for. Oh—before I forget, Karmele says you can come over in the morning to see the house."

"Thank you, Jacques."

They continued up the stairs before saying goodnight. Once Andrea was alone in the bedroom, she walked over to the dresser and reached for her cell phone to call her parents. They'd still be up.

After three rings she heard, "Bauers."

"Mom?"

"Andrea honey— Your dad and I were just talking about you. How are you?"

Avoiding the questions she said, "Tonight there was a family party. The gifts you sent were a huge success."

"Gabe gave me a list. It was fun to fill."

She grabbed the receiver tighter. "I couldn't believe it when I saw the King and Queen of Hearts. Mom—"

"I always intended to give them to you when you found the right man."

Andrea stifled a moan. "There's only one problem.

I—I'm not the right woman,'' she said in a strangled tone.

''What on earth are you talking about?''

''Oh, Mom... I've made such a terrible mistake.''

''What mistake is that?'' Her father's distinctive voice. He must have picked up another extension. How long had he been listening?

''Dad—''

''Tell us what's wrong, Andrea.''

''Everything.''

''Why don't you start with the part where you said you're not the right woman.''

''Gabe doesn't love me. He married me for another reason, and now that reason no longer exists.''

''Gabe isn't a man who makes any decision lightly, least of all when it comes to a matter as sacred as marriage.''

''Your father's right, honey. I never saw anyone so eager to be a husband.''

''That's because he thought he needed me.''

''And now he doesn't?''

''No.''

''Did he tell you that?'' her father questioned.

''He didn't have to. Tonight I learned the baby Jeanne-Marie miscarried wasn't Gabe's after all, so he no longer needs me to try to provide a replacement.''

After a long period of quiet on the other end her mother said, ''Who's Jeanne-Marie?''

''One of Gabe's sisters-in-law.''

''I think you'd better start at the beginning, honey.''

''You're not going to like it, Dad.''

''Let us be the judge of that.''

CHAPTER EIGHT

WHEN Gabe didn't see the car in front of the house where he'd been raised, he drove around the corner past Philippe's and Yves's. Still no luck.

Maybe his father had lingered at Helene's, but there was no sign of his car at either of his aunts' homes. Much as he would love to interrogate Cecile after what she'd revealed to Andrea, the information he required could only come from his own parent.

With two choices left to him, he cruised around the harbor's bars including the Petit Marin. Though determined to find his father no matter the place or hour, he had to admit he was relieved when he couldn't spot Giles's car anywhere.

That left the marina.

To Gabe's surprise, his search there didn't produce results, either.

Stymied for the moment, he looked out at the water shimmering beneath a full moon. There were few nights on St. Pierre as perfect as this one.

Was it possible his father had been attacked by a fit of melancholy and it had caused him to drive somewhere isolated on the island where he could drink himself into a stupor?

Gabe had watched him at the party. Giles had only drunk one glass of wine. Not enough to dull the pain of happy memories long since passed.

Though Gabe had only been married to Andrea less

than two weeks out of the six and a half months of knowing her, the thought of her ever leaving him made him physically ill. In that regard he could relate to his father's agony.

Instinct caused him to pick the drive to the isolated part of the island for one last search. As he rounded a curve, he spied his father's car parked on the shoulder. A medium-wave radio station had been built near the top of the hillside which gave a high view over the ocean. From that vantage point you could look down on the town.

After parking behind the Peugeot, Gabe levered himself from the car and hiked up the trail past the small building. As he reached the summit, he glimpsed his father's outline in the moonlight.

He looked so lonely standing there with his head down, his hands in his pockets, Gabe hurt for him. If he'd been drinking, there was no evidence of it.

"Papa?"

His parent jerked around in surprise. "Gabriel— Why aren't you home with your wife?" A mild sea breeze ruffled their hair and played havoc with their neckties.

Gabe undid his and stuffed it in his suit pocket. Then he moved closer to his father where he could see his features clearly and detect anything else revealing.

"Cecile said something to Andrea tonight that rocked my world."

Giles grimaced. "My sister was always difficult, even as a child. She has considered it her mission in life to hurt everyone I love. What can I do to help make things right for Andrea?"

His father's response wasn't at all what Gabe had expected. If Giles had something to hide, he was doing a hell of a job of it.

"I didn't ask you this question before, but I'm going to ask it now. How soon after I left the island did Jeanne-Marie tell you she was pregnant with my child?"

Giles eyed him soberly. "Yves was the one who came to me with the news the two of them were in love and wanted to get married."

Another shocker. Gabe's eyes closed tightly for a moment.

"After the bitter history between Evangeline's family and mine because I didn't marry her, the idea of her daughter becoming Yves's wife was almost unbearable to me."

Gabe could imagine.

"Hoping to dissuade your brother, I suggested that because he'd only been dating her a couple of months since his breakup with Suzette, it would be wise to give their relationship more time. I hated to see him get caught on the rebound."

"Is that when he admitted she was expecting?"

His father nodded. "I had a hard time believing it and told him I wanted to speak to Jeanne-Marie. He went to get her. To my chagrin, when they came back to the house, Evangeline was with them.

"She assured me they'd been to see Docteur LeBrun. Since her daughter was definitely pregnant, she demanded a date be set for their wedding. I had no choice but to go along with the arrangements.

"Then fate stepped in and Jeanne-Marie had a miscarriage. I again advised Yves to postpone the ceremony for a few months. Unfortunately he turned on me and accused me of hating Jeanne-Marie because of Evangeline.

"After losing your mother and not knowing how soon you would return to the island, the thought of Yves becoming estranged from me was too much. So I played the role of the happy father-in-law-to-be. A week before the wedding, I found Evangeline waiting for me by my car when I came in from a fishing run.

"The second I saw her, I knew in my gut there was trouble, but I never imagined what kind..." his voice grated.

"She told me Jeanne-Marie had always been in love with you, *mon fils,* that *you* were the baby's birth father, but you had rejected her. If I didn't keep you away from the wedding and their lives, she feared her daughter wouldn't go through with it, not after having lost your baby. Did I want another scandal all St. Pierre would be talking about for another fifty years?"

His father's face seemed to crumple in the moonlight.

"Evangeline told me there was no question about the paternity since she'd seen the two of you on the boat alone the night of the Basque festival. If I wanted proof about how far along Jeanne-Marie really was before the miscarriage, all I had to do was phone Dr. LeBrun.

"She warned me that if I didn't make sure you stayed away, she would tell Yves the truth herself. I knew she meant it because she has always wanted to hurt me for choosing your mother over her."

Mon Dieu. It was just as his grandfather had suspected.

"When I told you not to come to the wedding, I was only testing you, Gabriel. I fully expected you to deny any involvement with Jeanne-Marie. But you didn't defend yourself—" He groaned the last few words.

Gabe struggled to control his emotions. "I only slept with Jeanne-Marie one time. It was the night of the festival, the night you told me mother wasn't ever coming back."

His father's eyes flared with remembered pain.

"That night I went out to the trawler early and got drunk. Jeanne-Marie must have followed me. Evangeline was helping Karmele with the food. She *couldn't* have seen us together!

"It's all hazy, but at some point Jeanne-Marie did show up. At the time I didn't understand why."

"What do you mean?"

"I'm getting to that, Papa." He threw his head back. "I told her to go home, but she refused. She said she'd heard about the divorce from her mother and knew how close I was to Maman.

"One thing led to another. To be honest, I don't remember much about that night except that thanks to your talks with me, I did take precautions."

"That means she couldn't have gotten pregnant by *you!*" Giles cried out. His reaction was too raw not to be real. Gabe realized his father had been completely deceived.

He shook his head. "Not unless we were one of those couples who defied the statistics! At some point I fell asleep. When I woke up and found her still there, I couldn't believe what I'd done. It was almost one in the morning. Before I sent her packing, I apologized and told her to forget the whole experience since it was a huge mistake.''

''Is that why you left for New York two days later? Because you felt guilty? Evangeline said it was the reason.''

''No, Papa. Everything Evangeline told you was a lie from start to finish. I couldn't take it when you and Maman decided to get a divorce. It felt like my world had fallen apart. I had to get out of there.''

''Gabriel—'' His father looked stricken, making him appear years older than he was. ''What have I done to you?''

''Not you, Papa. Evangeline! She's the real culprit here and has been using her cohort Cecile to do her dirty work for years.''

He stepped closer, his lips tight. ''What did my sister say to Andrea tonight?'' he demanded.

''While Cecile was doing her best to run my wife off the island, Andrea set her back by claiming there was a question as to the paternity of Jeanne-Marie's baby. Andrea was referring to Yves of course.

''But Cecile didn't know that. She must have thought the jig was up because she let it slip that Claude was the one who'd got his own niece pregnant.''

His father staggered backward. ''Evangeline's brother— I remember he left the island at the same time you did.''

''That's right. God knows how long that sick pervert molested her, let alone how long Evangeline knew about it and never told anyone!

''Her master plan was to pin the pregnancy on me,

so she sent her daughter to New York after me, hoping she'd return with a ring on her finger.''

"Jeanne-Marie visited you in New York?" Giles sounded aghast.

"*Oui, Papa.* To her credit, she didn't tell me she was pregnant. She only said that she was in love with me and hoped I would come back to the island. I told her I wasn't interested, that she should go home and get on with her life. If I'd known she was pregnant, I would have stood by her though—and it wasn't ever my baby.''

By now his father looked livid. "It's all making sense now. When Jeanne-Marie couldn't have you, she made a play for Yves. No wonder Evangeline was afraid for you to show up at the wedding. You might have started asking too many questions, causing the plan to blow up in her face.''

Gabe nodded. "It was all Evangeline's doing. Jeanne-Marie probably felt so ashamed and guilty for something that wasn't her fault, her mother was able to manipulate her into doing whatever she was told. That girl needs psychiatric help.''

His father's eyes turned black with rage. "So does Evangeline. When she couldn't have me, she made certain she still had ties to me through her daughter.''

"Do you think Yves knows the truth?''

The two men stared at each other. "After what you've told me tonight, I have no idea. I do know one thing. They've made their marriage work and are devoted parents.''

"Then I'll never say anything to Yves. That's up to Jeanne-Marie.'' After a brief silence, "Did

Evangeline have something to do with the reason mother left?''

The answer was a long time in coming. "Indirectly. When Papa was going through hard times, I tried to help him so I looked for a second job. Evangeline told me her father would hire me because Claude hated fishing. So I went to work for him.

"As you know, he was one of the only well-to-do men on the island. He gave me a year's advance which I promptly handed over to Papa. I was naive enough to think he'd done it because he felt sorry for him, and knew I was good for the work.

"When I met your mother and realized I couldn't possibly marry Evangeline, her father fired me on the spot and told me I was to pay him back immediately with interest or he would press charges.

"There was no way I could do that unless I got help from an outside source. I didn't want Papa or your mother to know about it, so I applied for a business loan to raise mink for export. Once the money was in my hands, I paid Evangeline's father back every sou.

"Though I worked that job plus the fishing, we lived close to the poverty line for years because the mink business never took off. I had to pay the bank loan back and it drained us.

"At one of Cecile's parties, Evangeline was there. She chose that occasion to tell your mother my secret. When Carol found out the real reason why we'd had to struggle so long and hard, she was furious with me because her father would have given us a loan at the beginning.

"She accused me of letting my pride ruin our marriage. The next thing I knew, she announced she was divorcing me. It was the very action Evangeline had hoped for.

"Your mother said she wouldn't fight for you children because you all had fishing in your blood and wouldn't be happy anywhere else. Instead she would come to the island every month to stay close to you. Her visits have kept me from going under."

Incredible. "Have you ever asked her to come back for good?"

"No. She faced adversity every moment she lived with me. I didn't feel I had the right to ask for a second chance."

Gabe raked trembling hands through his hair. "We've both let pride ruin our lives, Papa. But no longer!"

"No longer," his father whispered before the two men hugged for a long time.

"I hope you meant that," Gabe finally said, "because I've got a new business proposition for you. One that can involve the whole family while the island's fishing grounds are being built up again. Andrea's the one who turned me on to the idea though she doesn't know it yet."

"Why don't you tell me about it while we walk back to our cars? Andrea must be wondering where you are. Don't make my mistake and take your wife for granted until it's too late."

"I don't intend to."

There was so much to tell Andrea, Gabe was fairly exploding with the need to talk to her when he returned to his grandfather's house. But for once she didn't wake up when he entered their bedroom. She was in too deep a sleep. He decided to forego a shower so he wouldn't disturb her.

What he wanted to share with her would have to wait until morning. To remove himself from temptation, he lay on his side away from her while his mind digested the earthshaking revelations that had come to light. At some point oblivion took over.

The morning started out with the sun shining as brightly as always. Andrea donned Levi's and a yellow cotton top for her trip to the harbor on Jacques's bike.

Though she was dying to know what had happened after Gabe had caught up with his father last night, she'd purposely left her husband in bed sleeping.

Now that the window of opportunity to conceive had passed, they could drop the act of being lovers. For the last couple of weeks he'd given the performance of his life in the passionate husband department.

If she wasn't pregnant, it wouldn't be because Gabe hadn't taken advantage of every possible minute to make it happen. But the time had come to give it a permanent rest.

She'd rather die than have Gabe think she expected those hours of ecstasy to continue. The effort on his part wasn't necessary now that she was no longer ovulating.

Nothing would turn him off more than to discover she'd fallen in love with him. All she had to do was remember his experience with Jeanne-Marie. Especially at this juncture when he'd just learned he hadn't fathered her baby after all. The new knowledge brought to light made her contract with Gabe null and void.

That was the other reason she'd wanted to get away from him this morning undetected. Andrea had a fear that when her husband awakened, he would feel obligated to take her on an inspection of Karmele's house after breakfast.

The last thing Andrea wanted was to see the inside of it and get all excited about fixing up their first home when she knew she wouldn't ever be living there with him.

The chances of her period coming in another week were close to a hundred percent. She would be a fool to carry this charade any further. Otherwise she would dream dreams that couldn't possibly come true. They would make her torment even more unbearable once she'd returned to her parents in Scarsdale.

Last night their advice not to do anything hasty or impulsive had prevented her from calling a taxi first thing this morning to take her to the airport. Barring that escape route, she'd decided to get in all the sightseeing to the other islands she could over the next week. Once she left St. Pierre, she knew in her heart of hearts she'd never be back.

When Jacques had seen her on the stairs this morning and learned of her plans to go exploring the town on her own, he'd told her she was welcome to take his bike if she was determined to leave the car for Gabe.

She gave him a hug and took him up on his offer, telling him she probably wouldn't be back until dinner. Since Gabe had wanted to spend some time with Fabrice today, it was the perfect opportunity for her to acquaint herself with some of the places they hadn't had time to visit yesterday.

Jacques had urged her to eat breakfast before she left, but she'd told him she would drop by one of the fabulous patisseries they'd walked past yesterday and indulge herself. The image of his smiling face as he waved her off stayed with her all the way into town.

Eyeing a *fruiterie* along the way, she rested the bike against the exterior of the shop and went inside. The beautiful produce made her mouth water for everything she saw. As she reached for a luscious-looking golden pear, she heard her name called and glanced over her shoulder.

It was the auburn haired teacher she'd met in Halifax before boarding the plane. "*Bonjour,* Marsha!"

The other woman smiled before she answered with the same greeting. "I can see you've become a serious French student already."

That was another dream Andrea needed to let go of, but she wasn't about to confess it. Marsha was under the impression Andrea was a starry-eyed newlywed who would be living the rest of her life here with her handsome French husband. Nothing could be further from the truth.

"I can say good morning, good evening and I'm delighted to meet you. That's the sum total of my repertoire!"

Her hazel eyes twinkled. "I'm impressed."

"Why aren't you with the other teachers?"

"We have the day off to do whatever we want. As you can see, my first thought was food."

"Great minds think alike," Andrea came back with

a smile as she walked to the counter to pay for her pear. Marsha followed with an apple in hand. They left the shop eating their fruit.

"Do you have to rush back to your husband?"

"No. He has plans to visit his best friend today, so I'm free, too. I borrowed his grandfather's bike and thought maybe I'd explore some of the other islands. Have you been to any of them?"

"Not yet. We'll be doing it on the weekend when we don't have to attend classes."

"Would you like to come with me?"

"I'd love it. There's a bike rental place for tourists near the hotel where we're staying. I'll get one. To be honest I much prefer going with a friend than being herded around like cattle."

"I know exactly what you mean. My husband gave me a personal tour of St. Pierre yesterday and—" Andrea broke off talking, disgusted with herself that thoughts of Gabe filled her mind to the exclusion of everything else. "Well, anyway, I enjoyed it."

"Who wouldn't?" her friend teased. "If I were married to a man like him, I wouldn't want to be with anyone else, either. Every woman on the tour talked about how gorgeous he was. Some of them took pictures of him."

"You're kidding!"

"No, I'm not." She shook her head emphatically. "In fact I dare say every one of them is downright jealous of you, including me," Marsha murmured with a wink.

Andrea groaned inwardly. Little did Marsha know how jealous Andrea already was of the woman who would win Gabe's heart one day.

She pulled the bike from the wall and walked it alongside Marsha as they made their way into the heart of town. A few doors down they passed a patisserie. Marsha darted inside to pick up some ham filled croissants.

By the time they reached the bike shop, they were full of pastry including *pain au chocolat* which they shared.

Once she had procured a bike, they headed for the ferry, stopping en route at an *épicerie* for bottled water. Andrea had to admit it was nice being with a warm, friendly, open woman from her own country.

More than ever she wondered how Gabe's mother had survived the hostility of her husband's insular family during the first months of their marriage. Naturally getting pregnant with Yves would have given her the focus she needed to shut out a lot of the pain, but still...

"What shall we do?" Marsha asked when they reached the dock. "Visit Sailor's Island, or Miquelon?"

"Gabe told me it's an hour's ferry ride to Miquelon. Since we've got the whole day, we could ride our bikes to Langlade from Miquelon and see both islands." *The longer I'm away from my husband, the better.*

"Sounds perfect to me."

"Good."

They bought their tickets and walked their bikes on board. In another twenty minutes the *Galante* got under way. There were quite a few tourists, mostly Canadians speaking French. Andrea and Marsha made up the smattering of Europeans and Americans, some of whom were standing at the railing by them.

As they headed out to sea riding the gentle swells, Andrea experienced the strangest sense of loss to see St. Pierre grow smaller until it was a mere hump on the horizon before it finally disappeared. Such a tiny, isolated spot of earth to have such a tentacle hold on her emotions!

But it was Gabe's home, not hers.

Wishing he weren't her obsession, she suggested they walk to the bow and watch for Miquelon to come into view. As they passed an American couple with children, she heard one of them say they couldn't wait to see the whales.

Andrea would love to spot them on this trip, too. Gabe had told her that one day soon he'd take her out in the open sea where she could view the spectacular sight through binoculars.

So many things he'd talked about them doing together, but that was before the illuminating conversation with Cecile last night which had changed everything.

"Andrea? Are you feeling seasick?"

She jerked her head toward Marsha. "No—are you?"

"A little. The wind has come up and the swells are getting worse." They *were* now that she thought about it. "You went a little pale just now, so I thought maybe you were suffering, too."

"I-it's probably because I'm struggling with a personal problem," she said honestly. "I'm sorry you're not feeling well."

"It's embarrassing to admit."

"Don't be absurd. You can't help it. We'll be there in twenty minutes. You can see land ahead. Keep staring at the horizon."

Five minutes later she followed her friend into the rest room where she proceeded to lose her breakfast. Marsha wasn't alone. There was a lineup for the toilettes. The poor things.

By the time they went ashore at the north end of the largest and longest of the islands, Marsha felt too sick to do anything but sit on the stone wall near the pier by their bikes for a while.

"The tour director warned us to take Dramamine if we were going to visit any islands, but I didn't think I would need it because I've been on boats before."

"You never know, Marsha. I'd always eaten peanuts without problem. Then last year I suddenly felt my lips and tongue swell. After a process of elimination, I discovered I was allergic to them. I couldn't believe it. Anyway, while you rest I'm going to find you some cola to help settle your stomach."

Andrea left her to cycle to the nearest store and bring back a couple of cans. After an hour her friend had recovered enough to ride her bike into the town of seven hundred people who Gabe said were mostly the descendants of Basques and Acadians.

During the time they'd been sitting there, clouds had blotted out the sun, and the famous fog he'd talked about moved inland from the ocean. They pedaled through dense pockets of it, but Andrea could tell her friend was too weak to keep up much longer.

"There's a small hotel straight ahead," she said. "We'll get a room for you." The fact that Marsha didn't protest spoke volumes.

Within five minutes their bikes had been secured by the concierge at the desk. They were shown to a room on the second floor reached by a circular flight of stairs. The whole layout was similar to the charming hotel Andrea had stayed at with Gabe in Champigny.

Remembering that evening brought a pang of longing for her husband so intense, Andrea was in literal pain. She and Marsha made a real pair. Her friend collapsed on one of the twin beds.

Andrea looked out the window trying to glimpse the ferry, but the fog was thick. She couldn't see much of anything.

"I'm so sorry," Marsha whispered. Her face looked like paste.

"Please don't say that again. Even if you weren't ill, we couldn't go anywhere until this soup dissipates. Try to sleep. That'll help you the most."

Andrea waited until her friend didn't need to run to the bathroom again, and had conked out. Then she slipped from the room.

After a talk with the concierge who told her the fog wasn't that bad and wouldn't prevent the ferry from going back to St. Pierre at four, she went to another patisserie for some rolls and little quiches. Hopefully when Marsha awakened, she would feel well enough to eat something.

But in that assumption, Andrea was wrong. Her friend slept till three-thirty, but was still too nauseated to try anything except cola. There was no way she would be able to go back on the ferry. The only solution was to stay overnight and put Marsha on a plane to St. Pierre tomorrow.

Before she went back to sleep again, Andrea got

the name of her hotel so she could inform her tour
director what had happened. Then she asked the op-
erator for the phone number of Jacques Corbin. She
knew Gabe's cell phone number, but chose not to use
it, hoping he wouldn't be at the house when she
called.

Luckily Jacques was home alone. He informed her
Gabe had gone out for lunch with Fabrice, but hadn't
come back yet.

That was good news. Andrea had hoped to put some
time and distance between her and her husband. Now
it seemed she was getting her wish.

After apprising Jacques of the situation, she gave
him the name of the hotel where they were staying,
and told him she would fly back with Marsha in the
morning. Under the circumstances Gabe and Fabrice
could spend the rest of the day and evening together
if they wanted.

Jacques muttered something to the effect that Gabe
hadn't been happy when he'd discovered she'd left
this morning without waking him up. The news that
she wouldn't be coming home at all was really going
to upset him, especially when she'd left her cell phone
behind so he couldn't reach her.

Andrea didn't believe Jacques. If anything, she
knew it was Gabe's grandfather who was disappointed. He loved to cook, and had probably been in
the process of preparing another delicious meal for
them when she'd called. Perhaps he'd asked Karmele
to join them for a farewell dinner together.

As for Gabe, he had to be feeling suffocated by his
claustrophobic togetherness with Andrea over the last
two weeks. She had no doubts he would breathe a sigh

of relief when he heard that fate had intervened to let him off the hook for the next eighteen hours.

Tonight he wouldn't have to play the part of the attentive, adoring husband who couldn't wait to get his wife in bed. He didn't know it yet, but the show was over.

Don't worry, my love. The second my period comes, I'll be gone. In the meantime, I'll find other ways to make certain you don't have to dance attendance on me anymore.

"Grand-père? I'm on my way home. Is Andrea there yet?"

When he heard what the old man had to say, Gabe felt the tight bands constricting his lungs relax. *Mon Dieu.* No wonder he hadn't been able to find her!

While she was stuck in a hotel room on Miquelon with a seasick friend, he and Fabrice had long since eaten lunch. For the last two hours they'd been driving around St. Pierre looking everywhere for her.

The pit in his gut had started that morning at the precise moment he'd reached for her in bed and discovered himself alone for the first time since their wedding ceremony.

His alarm grew when he realized she'd gone off without her cell phone, or a word to him. After he couldn't see any sign of her or the bike, he feared something was really wrong and asked Fabrice to excuse him.

Now that he'd been told where to find her, he could go after her.

It was providential that last year he'd funded the establishment of new heliports and copters on both islands to build tourism and help in emergencies. Little had he known then that he would need to avail himself of the service within days of arriving on St. Pierre.

Relieved to have learned his wife was staying at Le Mistral, he drove to the house to pack a bag for them. Considering her friend was too sick to go anywhere, he and Andrea would make up for that night in Champigny when he hadn't dared finish what he'd started on the dance floor.

At that point in time, one wrong move on his part could have made every dream of his go up in smoke.

Though he'd been on fire for her then, it was nothing compared to the conflagration going on inside of him now. Every time she welcomed him into her arms, he felt reborn.

Due to the fog, it was three hours later before the helicopter was cleared for flight. At eight o'clock he checked into the hotel on Miquelon. Once he'd taken the stairs two at a time to the next floor and put his suitcase in the room with a double bed, he walked down the hall and knocked on Andrea's door.

He was out of breath, but it wasn't because of exertion.

There was no answer. He knocked harder and longer, but it was evident they'd gone out. Maybe her friend was feeling better and they'd decided to eat at one of the local restaurants.

Rather than drive himself crazy trying to find the right one, he went back downstairs and read a newspaper in the lobby while he waited for his wife to appear.

An hour went by before he began to think Andrea's

friend might have needed treatment at the local clinic. The concierge gave him the number. Within minutes Gabe learned his hunch was right.

"Will you call me a taxi, *s'il vous plaît?*"

CHAPTER NINE

"ANDREA?"

At the hushed sound of the deep, familiar male voice coming from behind her, Andrea's heart almost flew out of its chest cavity. She jumped up from the chair where she'd been sitting by Marsha.

After another siege of sickness, her friend had finally fallen asleep while they'd given her an IV to hydrate her and take away her nausea.

But the sight of Gabe's tall, powerful body dressed in a black turtleneck and jeans molding his thighs took her breath and caused her thoughts to reel.

She shook her head incredulously. "How did you get here?" she whispered.

He drew closer and cupped her face in his hands. "A helicopter flew me in. You didn't think I was going to let you stay on this island alone tonight did you?"

She was powerless to stop the sensuous mouth that descended on hers. At the moment of contact, she felt something different about him. There was a hunger in Gabe he'd never exhibited before.

The fact that they were in a clinic didn't seem to matter to him. She had the impression that if she let this continue, he might just devour her in plain sight of the staff. Of Marsha.

Whatever the reason for this explosion of need on his part, it had to stop!

Maybe he was so happy to be let out of his eighteen-year prison, he didn't know where to go with his emotions. But he could have no comprehension of how painful this was for her.

When Andrea reflected, she remembered that a much younger Gabe had made love to Jeanne-Marie at the blackest point of his life. Though he'd done it for different reasons, Andrea imagined his lovemaking with the other woman had been just as fiery and intense.

Was it any wonder Jeanne-Marie had followed Gabe to New York? There was something so intoxicating about him, you could be swept away in the torrent and never be the same again.

But he hadn't loved Jeanne-Marie then, and he didn't love Andrea now. He'd never spoken the words.

That was because he couldn't!

Six months she'd worked for him. Six months—yet it had taken her going to him with her sob story before he saw a way that they both might benefit from marriage.

Bret had been right.

Gabe couldn't have become a billionaire without there being a ruthless side to his nature.

He *was* ruthless in the sense that he couldn't feel love for any woman. It had been burned out of him. Years ago Jeanne-Marie learned the painful truth in New York.

Andrea knew the truth in Paris.

When Gabe called her at the apartment to hear her answer to his proposal, her head told him no, but her heart walked out the door and down to the limo where

Benny was waiting. It was her heart, not her head, that went through with the marriage ceremony. Her heart that was dying with love for him right now.

She put her hands against his chest and slowly eased herself out of his embrace. He muttered a protest after relinquishing her mouth. She thought his breathing sounded ragged.

"How long will your friend have to be here?"

Andrea averted her eyes. "I don't know."

He massaged her upper arms with growing urgency. His masculine appeal was so potent, she swayed in place.

"Let's go back to the hotel, *mon amour.* I got us a room to ourselves. I'll leave my cell phone number so the doctor can call us when she's ready to be released."

"I can't, Gabe."

"Andrea—" He said her name in an aching whisper. "They've drugged her. She'll probably stay asleep until morning."

"Nevertheless I promised I wouldn't leave her. Marsha's in a strange place where there's no one familiar except me." She could feel the war going on inside her husband. "Why don't you go back to the hotel and get a good night's sleep?"

His body tautened. "Why do I sense you're trying to get rid of me?"

Perspiration broke out on her hairline. "Don't be ridiculous," she cried softly. "I only said that because there's no point in both of us staying awake all night."

He gave her a gentle shake. "You think I can go to sleep tonight knowing you're here?"

"I'm sorry you came all this way for nothing. It

might have been better if you'd stayed home with your grandfather."

A sharp intake of breath resounded in the cubicle before his hands fell to his sides and formed fists. "I'm your husband, Andrea. Where else would I be but here with you?

"For all I knew, you'd made up the story about your friend being seasick and it was *you* who'd had an attack of the *mal de mer*."

She swallowed hard. "As you can see, I'm fine."

"Thank God for that." A palpable tension throbbed between them. "Why didn't you wake me this morning and ask me to bring you here?"

"Because you were in such a deep sleep and looked so exhausted, I wouldn't have dreamed of disturbing you. I thought I'd take a bike ride until you were up. But then I bumped into Marsha and we decided to go on the ferry. It was a spur-of-the-moment decision."

After a long silence, "Andrea—have I done something to offend you?"

"Of course not."

He put a finger under her chin and forced her to look at him. "Do you swear it?" he demanded.

"Do I have to swear to you in order for you to believe me?" She didn't flinch as she asked the question.

A glint of some unnamed emotion came and went in his eyes before they became veiled so she couldn't read their expression.

"Would you prefer I left you alone?"

Oh Gabe, her heart cried. "I wouldn't want you to do anything you don't feel like doing."

He traced the outline of her lips with his fingers.

"You're the one who looks exhausted now," he murmured before removing his hand. "Sit back down and I'll keep the vigil with you."

In an economy of movement he snagged a stool from the corner and planted his hard-muscled body next to her.

"Did you talk to your father last night?" she asked when she couldn't bear the painful atmosphere between them another second.

She was the one responsible for the drastic change in Gabe's behavior now. It pained her he'd reverted to that aloof, moody part of him she hadn't seen for a while.

"We talked. My parents and Jeanne-Marie were victims of Evangeline's sickness. But all the secrets are out now. She won't be able to hurt any of us again."

"Does that mean you can be close to your family now?"

"Yes. In ways it's going to be better than before."

"Even with Yves?"

He nodded. "My brother believes the baby was his, and that's the way it's going to stay."

Tears stung her eyes. "I'm so glad, Gabe."

"Are you?" he fired the question so fast she was stunned.

Andrea jerked her head around. "How can you ask me that?"

His jaw hardened. "Maybe because you weren't there this morning wanting to know."

"I told you why I left."

His stormy gray gaze pierced hers. "Then I guess we both have our answer."

She'd hurt him. She'd hurt him in a way that cut to the soul. The horror of it was, she couldn't reverse time. You didn't get a second chance to do it right. The moment was gone forever.

Gabe had needed to share the most important thing in his life with her, but she'd been asleep when he'd come home, and she'd left before he'd awakened. She'd done what she'd had to do for self-preservation, but a part of her would never forgive herself for causing him more pain.

For the rest of the night Gabe sat in brooding silence while Andrea rested her head against the back of the chair. She was afraid to say anything that would make matters worse. But nothing could be worse than the dreadful silence between them.

They watched the staff come in on a periodic basis to check on their patient and take her vital signs. Around five in the morning Marsha woke up feeling well enough to talk with Andrea and Gabe. She even asked for some juice to drink.

By six she could keep down the roll they brought her. The doctor came in at six-thirty and said she could go home as soon as she felt well enough to leave.

Gabe rose to his feet. "While you girls stay here, I'll get a taxi back to the hotel and pack up anything you left in the room. I'll arrange for your bikes to be taken to the heliport. Then I'll come back for you and we'll fly home."

Marsha sat on the side of the hospital bed and squeezed both their hands. "Thank you for everything you've done. I'm so grateful you can't imagine. Your wife is an angel."

Gabe flashed Marsha a heart-stopping smile. "My grandfather says the same thing."

But you'll never think that will you, my love.

The shadows beneath his eyes and a noticeable growth of beard only seemed to enhance his dark, incredibly attractive features.

Andrea handed him the key to their hotel room, then hurriedly looked away so he wouldn't catch her devouring him with her eyes.

Within an hour and a half, they were back on St. Pierre. The fog had dissipated. It was going to be a beautiful day.

Marsha was still a little unsteady. Gabe helped her into the Nissan. When they reached the hotel where she was staying with her tour group, both Andrea and Gabe walked her inside. The director had been waiting for her and took over.

After hugs and promises to stay in touch, Andrea followed her husband out to the car. He stopped at the bike shop to return Marsha's rental, then they drove home.

When they walked in the house Jacques was there to greet them. His anxious eyes studied their faces. "Neither of you looks like you've had any sleep."

Gabe rubbed the side of his firm jaw. It made a rasping sound. "You're right about that, Grand-père."

"Then you'd better go to bed because we're having someone very special for dinner this evening."

"Karmele?" her husband asked before she could.

"No. Your maman."

Andrea almost moaned her agony aloud.

She didn't want to meet Gabe's mother, not when

Andrea was leaving him in another week. How could she possibly face her now?

"I thought she wasn't coming until July." By the tone of Gabe's voice, Andrea couldn't tell how he felt about the news.

"She missed your wedding. I guess she didn't want to wait that long to welcome her daughter-in-law to the family."

The room started to spin.

Gabe picked Andrea up in his strong arms. She heard him say *bonne nuit* to his grandfather before he started for the stairs. The last thing she remembered was the tender kiss he pressed to her lips before covering her with the quilt.

When Andrea suddenly came wide awake, it was after six p.m. She let out a gasp and sat up in the bed. She'd been asleep close to nine hours. She couldn't remember the last time she'd slept this long. Not since high school anyway.

Had Gabe's mother already arrived? Was that why he wasn't still in bed, too?

She flung off her covers and dashed into the bathroom to shower and wash her hair.

What to wear? Which outfit should she put on to meet her? Would it matter to Gabe?

After changing her mind half a dozen times, Andrea opted for her champagne colored silk blouse and matching pleated pants. They were dressy, but not as formal as the black dress she'd worn to the party.

By the time she was ready to go downstairs, her body was shaking with a dichotomy of emotions and feelings. They ranged from abject fear to an exploding curiosity about the woman whose decision to divorce her husband had devastated Gabe at such a critical time in his development.

Voices drifted into the foyer. One of them was female. Taking a deep breath, Andrea walked in the living room.

She discovered Giles standing there with Gabe and Jacques. All three of them were conversing with a stunning brunette woman dressed in a two-piece melon colored suit. She had light gray eyes and was almost as tall as her ex-husband.

If she was this lovely in her fifties, Andrea could imagine what a beauty she must have been at nineteen. When she smiled, it was Gabe's smile.

Just seeing her standing there by her son explained so much about him. All the missing pieces of the puzzle seemed to fall into place faster than she could fit them.

His eyes locked with hers before he strode toward her. He put his arm around her waist and drew her closer. "Mother? I'd like you to meet my wife. Andrea? This is my mother, Carol."

"Hello," they both said tentatively. Then they laughed. The moment was so nerve-racking and amusing at the same time, it broke the ice.

Carol reached for her and hugged her hard. Her eyes glazed over with tears. "Do you have any idea how nice it is to have one daughter-in-law who comes from my part of the planet?"

She exuded that unstinting warmth she'd bequeathed to Bertrand and Philippe. Andrea loved her already. No wonder Giles had lost his heart to her. His ex-wife was so open and friendly, she would have come as a complete shock to the Corbin women who didn't have it in their genes to be as demonstrative.

"You're a wonderful surprise, too," Andrea confessed in a tremulous voice.

Carol caught hold of her hands. "I'm so glad you feel that way. Forgive me for not coming to your wedding. Gabe assures me he told you I was in Florida with my sister and her family when he left the message on my voice mail."

"He did."

"That's good, because nothing could have kept me away otherwise. I'm envious of your parents and can't wait to meet them."

Giles nodded. "I'm looking forward to meeting them, too."

"We'll arrange it as soon as possible, won't we, *mon coeur*," Gabe declared.

Stop. Don't say anything else. I can't bear it.

"The salmon roast is waiting," Jacques murmured, almost as if he could feel Andrea's distress and wanted to help her. "Shall we go in the kitchen?"

Gabe took the initiative to usher her through the house. When they assembled around the kitchen table, Carol sat at her other side. Once they were served, everyone contributed to the conversation that concentrated on the outstanding meal and the latest news about family.

Carol seemed like any typical mother and grandmother who was totally interested in her offspring and grandchildren. Why on earth had she divorced Giles when it was obvious her family was her whole world?

But the moment the question entered Andrea's mind, she remembered that in another week people were going to be asking the same question about her. How come she'd left Gabe when it appeared they were so much in love?

It seemed the old adage still held true that "nobody knows what goes on behind closed doors except the two people involved."

After Gabe had downed a couple of juicy peaches for dessert, he grasped Andrea's hand before eyeing his mother. "I realize you always stay with Yves or Philippe while you're here, but we want a turn."

Jacques nodded.

"I'm afraid that's not going to happen," Giles interjected, drawing everyone's attention. To Andrea's shock, he slid an arm around Carol's shoulders, drawing her close in a possessive move reminiscent of the way Gabe sometimes held Andrea.

The unprecedented gesture had the effect of sending a charge of electricity through the air. While a look of total disbelief spread across Gabe's face, his grandfather sat there with a smile that lit up his eyes.

"Thanks to Andrea's conversation with Cecile the other night, Gabe and I were able to talk frankly about the past and clear up years of misunderstandings. Though Evangeline and her father did their best to ruin a lot of lives, we agreed that pride has been the downfall of the Corbin family.

"After our talk, I went home and phoned Carol to ask her forgiveness for putting her through hell when we first got married. I was a fool." His voice trembled.

Andrea lowered her head. Because she hadn't been there for Gabe to talk to yesterday morning, she didn't know what hell Giles was referring to.

"No more than I," Carol murmured. "What your father is trying to tell you, Gabe, is that as soon he opened up to me, I begged his forgiveness for not understanding him when he needed understanding the most. We were both idiots."

"That's a fact," Giles concurred. "Nevertheless she'll be staying with me from now on because we're getting remarried as soon as possible."

Andrea figured she wouldn't have a hand left after Gabe finished squeezing it, but right now that wasn't important. His joy had to be indescribable. She could only imagine the happiness this news was going to bring to their other children and grandchildren.

"Do my brothers know?" Gabe's voice was so husky, Andrea hardly recognized it.

"Not yet." His father seemed equally affected by overwhelming emotions. He sounded too choked up to talk. "We wanted to tell you first since you're the reason this miracle has come to pass."

"It's true, darling," his mother assured Gabe when he slowly shook his head. "Because you came back home, it triggered a series of events that have given this family a second chance at happiness."

Gabe's silvery gaze swerved to Andrea. "My wife has been the catalyst for everything that has happened."

Giles smiled at her. "Of course she has. She's remarkable, just like your mother. With both our wives living on the island now, Cecile's never going to be the same again," he chuckled.

Carol looked ecstatic. "Guess what? I'm buying us a new house!"

"We're giving the old one to Bertrand," Giles informed them.

"Yes, and we've decided to go into the business you were talking to your father about, Gabe."

"What business?" Andrea blurted. She couldn't stand to be in the dark any longer.

He stared at her through shuttered eyes. "The one you discussed with me during our flight from Halifax to St. Pierre."

Andrea's delicately arched brows frowned. "I don't rememb— Oh! You mean a tour business that brings students to the islands for French homestays?"

"That's the one."

Andrea blinked. "I didn't think you were even listening."

Everyone at the table chuckled. "I took it all in, *mon amour*," he said, making slow circles against her wrist with his thumb. "You were full of brilliant ideas after you talked to Marsha. I sat there in absolute awe of you."

His words brought a blush to her cheeks.

Jacques cocked his head. "Wasn't she the woman who got seasick yesterday?"

"Yes. She made the comment that it would be wonderful to bring language students here. I started thinking that if I'd had an opportunity to come to a place like this when I was in high school, I would have worked hard and saved my money just to have the experience."

"It's an excellent idea." Giles sounded excited. "We could run a program year round. With Carol's connections in the travel business, and mine among the fishermen here on the island, there's no telling what could develop. The one thing we do know is that it would bring in badly needed tourist dollars to every family wanting to be a host."

"You wouldn't have any problem finding students to sign up," Andrea spouted with enthusiasm. "In fact you'd probably end up turning people away. Yesterday on the ferry, this cute little boy was literally jumping up and down waiting to spot a whale.

"If I knew I were coming on a homestay to learn French and be able to go whale watching at the same time, I'd opt for that experience instead of the ones to Montreal or Quebec. This place has things to offer you can't find anywhere else unless you go to the Galápagos Islands.

"The beauty of St. Pierre et Miquelon is that it's so close to the continent," she said, warming to her subject. "It doesn't require a flight over an ocean. Students can come here by ferry from Newfoundland if they want. You don't have to have vaccinations or eat strange foods—all those things parents worry about for their teenagers.

"With all the Basque culture here, the students could have a choice whether they wanted to learn French or Euskarria. And I was thinking how exciting it would be for students who've never been around water or deep sea fishing trawlers. Imagine what an adventure it would be for guys in particular!"

The way everyone was looking at her, especially Gabe whose eyes gleamed with a mysterious light, she realized she'd babbled far too long and furiously.

"I think we've already found our program director, don't you, *mon trésor?*" Giles said out loud, though he'd addressed Carol.

She nodded. "I can't think of another person who would be more perfect. With your background as a computer software engineer, there's no end to the possibilities if we advertised over the Internet. The whole family can get involved if they want."

"We need to move with the times if St. Pierre is to have a future," Gabe's father said in a more serious vein.

His comment helped to take the onus off Andrea who didn't have the heart to tell them she wouldn't be here after next week. She would leave that to Gabe.

"I'm afraid the great days of fishing are behind us."

Gabe sat forward. "For now anyway, Papa. One day when these waters are repopulated, who knows? The key is to diversify."

Andrea watched him studying his parents as if he still couldn't believe their news. Neither could she. But the proof was before her eyes. Their love had never died. In that regard the two of them reminded her of her own parents. Still lovers as well as friends.

"Are you getting married at the church?" Gabe questioned.

His father nodded. "The same place we took our vows before. This time you boys can watch."

Carol laughed. "Father Cluny will have a fit."

"*Oh là là.*" Giles made a typical French gesture with his hand for Andrea's benefit, causing her to laugh. She loved their sense of fun.

"We'd better leave if we plan on seeing him tonight." He helped his wife up from the table.

"Giles darling—before we drive to the church, we

need to drop by the boys' houses and tell them our news. First, though, we'll help with the dishes."

The old man moved fast. He rushed around and kissed his daughter-in-law. "You two run along. I've got helpers."

"You're sure?"

"Positive." Gabe put his arms around both parents and embraced them. Andrea waited until everyone moved to the front door.

Carol turned to her. "It'll be a small wedding, but there's still a lot to do. We'll need all the help we can get. Let's do lunch tomorrow. I'll call you."

"I'd like that."

"Good."

Both of them hugged her. A side glance at Giles revealed a completely different man than the one she'd met a few days ago. It was as if he'd thrown off the heavy burden weighing him down. He even walked differently. A real miracle had happened!

The announcement of unexpected wedding plans couldn't have come at a better time for Andrea. With the focus on Gabe's parents, she had every excuse in the world to put off doing anything about Karmele's house. She didn't want to hear her husband's ideas for the nursery she knew he had in mind.

While Gabe and Jacques walked them out to the car, Andrea cleared the table. He kept such a neat house, there wasn't anything to do except load the dishwasher.

As she wiped off the counter, the kitchen phone rang. Since the men were still outside, she answered it.

"Andrea? I'm so glad I caught you home!" It was Marsha.

"You sound a lot better."

"I am. Believe me. When we left for the clinic, I thought I was going to die. I've never been that sick in my life!"

"I wanted to help you, but didn't know how."

"You were wonderful. So was your husband. How would you like to go out to dinner with me tomorrow night? That is if you're free. It's my way of thanking you."

"I'd love it!" Andrea meant it. The more things she had to occupy her time, the easier it would be to stay away from Gabe. "While we're together, I'd like to talk to you about a business proposition my husband's parents have in mind."

"What do you mean?"

"Well…be thinking about getting a bunch of your French students to come to St. Pierre for a homestay."

"You're kidding! Have you and your husband talked about being hosts?"

"No," Andrea answered honestly. "I—I won't be living on the island after next week."

A long silence ensued. "Don't tell me you and your husband are having marital problems—"

Andrea pressed a hand against her heart to stifle the paralyzing pain. That's when she felt the hairs prickling on the back of her neck. She sensed she wasn't alone.

Turning her head, she discovered Gabe's powerful physique filling the doorway. But nothing else was familiar. The light in his eyes had been extinguished.

His handsome features looked like they'd been carved from stone.

Her breathing constricted. "Marsha? I have to hang up, but I'll call you tomorrow." With a trembling hand she put the receiver on the hook.

"How long have you been standing there?"

"Long enough," his voice grated.

She hugged her arms to her waist. "Where's Jacques?"

"He went with the folks. We're finally alone and there's no place for you to run."

Panic set off an adrenaline attack. "I'm not sure I understand."

"Don't, Andrea," he bit out. "It isn't worthy of you. Last night I asked if I had offended you. You answered me with another question." After a tense pause, "I'm not going to let you get away with that tonight."

She avoided his rapier gaze.

"Do you have any idea how I felt when I came in here just now and overheard you telling a virtual stranger that you won't be here after next week? Surely your own husband had a right to know about it first!"

A shudder passed through her body. "I was going to tell you, Gabe. I swear it."

"Let's leave the swearing out of it, shall we?" he fired back, barely tamping down his rage. "I asked you to marry me. You said yes. We agreed not to worry about the future until we'd given it six months to try to get you pregnant."

"That's true. But everything has changed now that we know Jeanne-Marie didn't lose your baby."

"In what way?" he thundered.

"In *every* way—" she cried. "The reason you wanted to marry me no longer exists. All these years you've struggled with guilt because you believed you'd let down Jeanne-Marie when she needed you most. Now you know differently.

"You've been freed of that terrible burden and can live out the rest of your life with a clear conscience. After next week, I'll free you of your commitment to me. At long last you'll be able to look for love until you find it with the right woman, babies or no babies."

A sound like ripping silk escaped his throat. "Our contract was for six months."

To hear him bring up that word was a lethal blow. "You're a very gallant man, Gabe, but your sacrifice isn't necessary because we know the real truth about Jeanne-Marie."

Lines marred his face, aging him. "If that's the case, then why not leave me tonight? What's so sacred about next week?" He was livid.

"My period is due then," her voice throbbed. "As we both know, the chance that I'm pregnant is about a zillion to one.

"However—" She moistened her lips nervously. "Should I defy the odds of a woman riddled with endometriosis and we discover we're going to have a baby, then of course I won't be leaving. That part of the contract I intend to keep in the event we find out we're going to be parents."

His lips tautened. "You couldn't want a baby very badly if you're willing to give up after one month."

Gathering every bit of courage, she decided to lay

it on the line. "It takes a lot of hard work when you're not in love."

With her heart pounding like a war drum, she waited for him to tell her he loved her.

A tiny nerve pulsated at the corner of his mouth. "I'm going out, and don't know when I'll be back."

In seconds Andrea heard the front door open and close. She ran to the living room window in time to watch the car drive away.

Could death be any worse than this?

CHAPTER TEN

"GABRIEL? *Tu es là?*" Fabrice called out.

Gabe could see his friend's outline in the distance. *"Oui, mon ami."*

"I came as soon as I delivered my last fare." He jumped onto the trawler.

"Lise won't mind?" He untied the ropes before going into the wheelhouse. Fabrice followed him.

"No. She and the kids are at her mother's. When I listened to your message on my cell phone, I told her I wouldn't be home until morning."

There was no one like Fabrice. Gabe had always been able to count on him. "Let's go."

After turning on the headlights, he moved the boat out of the harbor at a wakeless speed.

"You handle the *Alouette* as if you'd never been away."

"But she responds like an old woman on her death bed. I've ordered a new one from Norway. It'll be here next week.

"I was wondering how I was going to give it to Papa without him turning me down. However after the events of the last forty-eight hours, I no longer have to worry about it."

"That sounds cryptic."

"After all these years *mes parents* have settled their differences. Would you believe they're going to be married next week at the church?"

Fabrice shook his head. "No. I don't believe it."

"I'm inviting you to the ceremony. When you come, you'll know I was speaking the truth. I've decided to give them the new boat for a wedding present."

Fabrice paced the floor for several minutes. "All right. I believe you. Since the news should have made a new man of you, then I take it Andrea has found out she's not pregnant yet."

Gabe grimaced. "We won't know about that for another week or more."

His friend blew air from his lips. "I've got all night. Take your time." He stretched out on the banquette with his arms folded.

The mournful sound of a buoy marking the channel reached his ears at some distance behind the trawler. Gabe shut off the motor and let the swells do the work.

He turned to Fabrice. "She doesn't love me."

"She said that to your face?"

"Not in those exact words."

"I want to hear what she did say. Exactly."

Gabe obliged him.

"Let me see if I've got your history straight. You both decided to get married without a word of love passing between you."

"I didn't dare tell her how I felt. She would never have believed me. But because of her medical condition, there wasn't time for courtship so I threw in my story about Jeanne-Marie for the leverage I needed."

"It *worked*."

"Not any longer. I'm going to lose her, Fabrice."

He cocked his head. "If she didn't love you in the

first place, then she was never yours to lose. Come on, Gabriel. Hasn't it occurred to you she might have married you because she loved you?"

"She would've told me. Andrea's not a liar."

"No?" he mocked. "Your wife's a brilliant woman. That's worse. I'd say you've met your match. You know what I would do if I were you?"

The pain was ripping him apart. "I don't want to hear it."

"Go home and call her bluff. Tell her you love her, and that you know she loves you, too."

"Just like that?" he ground out.

"Just like that. You're a gambler, otherwise you wouldn't have given away your billion dollars. What's another gamble at this stage in the game? You pulled off the biggest coup of your life when you got her to marry you.

"Then again, maybe it was Andrea who used her threat to quit the company as leverage to reel you in. The biggest fish in the sea. The granddaddy that's never been caught."

Gabe's heart gave a great kick. "If I thought that were true…"

"How many women do you know besides Andrea who would be glad to hear you weren't a billionaire anymore, *mon ami?*"

"None."

"Voilà!" He leaned forward until he was in Gabe's face. "And think about this—how many of them would agree to come to some strange little island nobody knows about, sight unseen, to live out the rest of their lives *if* it weren't for love? Answer me that if you can," he baited him.

"You should have been a prosecuting attorney."

"I'm not bad, am I," he said without a shred of humility.

In spite of Gabe's turmoil, a bark of laughter escaped. He turned on the motor and they headed back to the island.

After several hours of soul-searching, Andrea had taken a chair out to the front porch to wait for Gabe in the dark.

Jacques had never come home. She didn't know if he'd had a reason for staying away on purpose or not. If he'd wanted to give the two of them time alone, it was a wasted effort. Her watch said ten to two in the morning. There was still no sign of Gabe's car.

She suspected he'd gone to see Fabrice. The two of them could be anywhere. He'd told her they'd been known to put away more than a few bottles of beer in their time. In the mood he was in when he left, Andrea wouldn't be surprised if that was exactly what they were doing.

What a tragic irony that on the night he'd heard the wonderful news his parents were getting back together, he'd had to walk in the kitchen at the exact moment she'd told Marsha something never meant for his ears. At least not until Andrea was ready to tell him.

Too bad she didn't have a car or she would go to Fabrice's house and ask his wife where they'd gone. Andrea needed to make her confession. She couldn't live with herself any longer.

Once Gabe knew the truth, at least then he would

understand her behavior over the last few days and not hate her quite as much.

The breeze off the ocean was a little cooler now. She hurried in the house for a wrap. When she opened the front door to go back out on the porch, she almost collided with her husband.

He put out his hands to steady her. "What are you doing up at this hour still dressed?"

His voice sounded concerned, not angry. Whatever else he'd been doing, he hadn't been drinking, which came as another surprise.

"Waiting for you to come home."

"Why?"

"Because I need to tell you something. Until I do, I won't have any peace."

"There's something I have to tell you, too," he admitted rather emotionally. His hands moved up and down her arms with restless energy. She could feel their heat through her sweater. "There's only one reason I asked you to marry me. Surely by now you know what it is."

The world stood still.

She might have lied to herself about many things, but she'd never dared to believe the impossible. Not until this moment...

"It's the only reason why I accepted."

"You're in love with me!" His triumphant cry was loud enough for Karmele to hear.

"Yes, darling. Oh, yes! For such a long time. It happened at the interview."

"I know," he whispered against her lips. "I was there, remember? You brought a force into my office that knocked me sideways. It actually terrified me because I sensed this was it. You were the woman meant for me. What if I made a mistake and frightened you off before I could get you to fall in love with me?

"So I played it cool, biding my time."

Andrea covered his face in kisses. "You bided too much time! It was either leave the company or try to force myself to love someone else."

"When I heard you were with Bret—" His fingers tightened in her silken hair. "I swear I almost lost my mind."

"I *did* lose mine," she admitted, looping her arms around his neck. "There came a point when I realized I had to get away. I thought the six-week recuperation period would either cure me of Gabe Corbin's disease, or I would have found the strength to look for another job."

He flashed her the smile that always made her body feel like she was floating above the world.

"Gabe Corbin's disease— I like the sound of that."

"It's chronic you know." She pressed an avid kiss to his gorgeous male mouth. "I'm always going to suffer from it. My doctor told me the condition would grow worse over the years. There's no cure. You need to know about that up front."

"You need to know something up front too, *mon amour.* One way or another, we'll have children. If we find a hysterectomy is called for, then so be it. We'll adopt."

"Oh, Gabe—" Andrea crushed him in her arms, so deliriously happy she couldn't contain it.

"I have one favor to ask," he whispered into her hair.

"Anything!"

"Let's make it a double wedding. I want to say my vows to you in front of God and my family."

She hugged him tighter. "I was dreaming about that earlier tonight while I was sitting on the porch waiting for you to come home to me."

"I wondered what the living room chair was doing out here." He picked her up in his arms. "I had plans for us last night, but they were thwarted. Come on, *mon épouse delectable*. It's time we were both in bed where we belong. I have a hunger for you that won't wait any longer."

Father Cluny's raisin dark eyes looked at both of them with mild accusation.

"A marriage performed at a courthouse by a judge is no marriage."

"It is after a fashion, Father. But now Andrea and I want to do it right. Will you perform the honors after you marry my parents?"

His gray head reared back, the better to look at them. "This is all highly irregular. If Carol had stayed where she belonged, and *you* hadn't run off to build foundations in the sand, none of this would be necessary."

Gabe's arm tightened around Andrea's hip. "I found my rock on that sand, Father. Now I'm holding on to her for dear life."

He grunted, but it was an approving sound. Andrea like him in spite of his rough, Gallic edge.

"Am I going to have to remarry you two later on down the road, or do you think you've learned from your papa's disastrous mistake and this is it?"

"This is it!" Andrea declared in a strong voice.

"All four of us have repented of the sin of the pride. We've sworn never to let it be a stumbling block again."

The priest sat back and patted his stomach. The sweetest smile she'd ever seen suddenly broke out on his weathered face.

"I'll do it. Do you want the mass in English or French?"

"Maybe a little of both?" she suggested. "I'm learning the language as fast as I can, but these things take time."

Two weeks later the bell rang from the church tower as family and friends of the wedding party walked through the heart of St. Pierre to the Trois Fleurs restaurant which had been preparing for the festivities.

The two brides wore *peau-de-soie* wedding dresses. Andrea chose cream, Gabe's mother looked stunning in white. Twin mantilla's, Corbin family heirlooms of old French lace, adorned their heads. The grooms had donned matching black tuxes.

Andrea felt like she was in a dream. Gabe's fingers entwined tightly with hers in a possessive hold, letting all the world know she was his wife. He looked ten years younger today, and was the cynosure of every female eye.

Her parents walked behind them so her mother could keep her train from dragging on the ground. The sun shone from a clear blue sky. It couldn't have been a more glorious day. Andrea felt like she was going to burst from too much joy.

But the second they entered the restaurant and she breathed in the first aroma of fish which had been prepared for their wedding feast, she experienced another sensation of nausea, stronger than the wave that had washed over her during the wedding ceremony.

At first she tried not to let it bother her, but once Gabe had seated her at the head table, the unpleasant feeling persisted worse than ever. By the time she saw the heaping platters of oysters being brought to the table, she feared she was going to be ill like Marsha.

"Mom?" She leaned toward her mother and whispered, "I'm sick to my stomach."

"How wonderful!" her mother exclaimed in a hushed tone. "Your period's a week past due. I suffered horrible morning sickness almost from the moment you were conceived. You must be pregnant."

"Mom!"

"Come on. I'll help you to the rest room. I often had to eat two meals back to back in the morning during the first trimester. I'm afraid you're just like me."

"Andrea?" Gabe said in a alarm. "What's wrong, *mon coeur?* Your face looks like parchment."

But Andrea couldn't talk. She was too worried she wouldn't make it to the bathroom in time.

"Nothing's wrong," she heard her mother tell him. "It looks like you're going to be a father. Congratulations, Papa!"

Harlequin Romance®

HIS HEIRESS WIFE

by international bestselling author

Margaret Way

On sale next month in Harlequin Romance

Welcome to the intensely emotional world of Margaret Way, where rugged, brooding bachelors meet their match in the tropical heat of Australia....

In *His Heiress Wife* (HR #3811), meet Olivia Linfield, the beautiful heiress, and Jason Corey, the boy from the wrong side of the tracks made good. They should have had the wedding of the decade—except it never took place. Seven years later Olivia returns to Queensland to discover Jason installed as estate manager. Will Jason manage to persuade the woman he loved and lost how much he still wants her—and always has...?

*Starting in September,
Harlequin Romance has a fresh new look!
Available wherever Harlequin books are sold.*

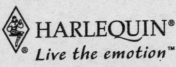

HARLEQUIN®
Live the emotion™

www.eHarlequin.com   HRHWMW

Harlequin Romance®

A compelling miniseries from Harlequin Romance

Contract Brides

From paper marriage...to wedded bliss?

A wedding dilemma:

What should a sexy, successful bachelor do if he's too busy making millions to find a wife, or finds the perfect woman and just has to strike a bridal bargain...?

The perfect proposal:

The solution? For better, for worse, these grooms in a hurry have decided to sign, seal and deliver the ultimate marriage contract...to buy a bride!

Don't miss the latest CONTRACT BRIDES story coming next month by emotional author Barbara McMahon.

Her captivating style and believable characters will leave your romance senses tingling!

September—Marriage in Name Only (HR #3813)

Starting in September,
Harlequin Romance has a fresh new look!

Available wherever Harlequin books are sold.

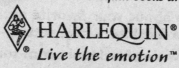

HARLEQUIN®
® *Live the emotion*™

www.eHarlequin.com

HRBMMINO

eHARLEQUIN.com

Your favorite authors are just a click away at www.eHarlequin.com!

- Take our **Sister Author Quiz** and we'll match you up with the author most like you!

- Choose from over 500 author **profiles!**

- Chat with your favorite authors on our **message boards.**

- Are you an author in the making? Get advice from published authors in **The Inside Scoop!**

- Get the latest on **author appearances** and tours!

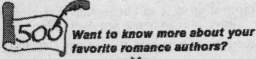

Want to know more about your favorite romance authors?

Choose from over 500 author profiles!

Learn about your favorite authors in a fun, interactive setting— visit www.eHarlequin.com today!

INTAUTH

If you enjoyed what you just read,
then we've got an offer you can't resist!

Take 2 bestselling love stories FREE!

Plus get a FREE surprise gift!

Clip this page and mail it to Harlequin Reader Service®

IN U.S.A.	IN CANADA
3010 Walden Ave.	P.O. Box 609
P.O. Box 1867	Fort Erie, Ontario
Buffalo, N.Y. 14240-1867	L2A 5X3

YES! Please send me 2 free Harlequin Romance® novels and my free surprise gift. After receiving them, if I don't wish to receive anymore, I can return the shipping statement marked cancel. If I don't cancel, I will receive 6 brand-new novels every month, before they're available in stores! In the U.S.A., bill me at the bargain price of $3.57 plus 25¢ shipping & handling per book and applicable sales tax, if any*. In Canada, bill me at the bargain price of $4.05 plus 25¢ shipping & handling per book and applicable taxes**. That's the complete price and a savings of 10% off the cover prices—what a great deal! I understand that accepting the 2 free books and gift places me under no obligation ever to buy any books. I can always return a shipment and cancel at any time. Even if I never buy another book from Harlequin, the 2 free books and gift are mine to keep forever.

186 HDN DZ72
386 HDN DZ73

Name _____ (PLEASE PRINT)

Address _____ Apt.# _____

City _____ State/Prov. _____ Zip/Postal Code _____

* Terms and prices subject to change without notice. Sales tax applicable in N.Y.
** Canadian residents will be charged applicable provincial taxes and GST.
All orders subject to approval. Offer limited to one per household and not valid to current Harlequin Romance® subscribers.
® are registered trademarks owned and used by the trademark owner and or its licensee.

HROM04 ©2004 Harlequin Enterprises Limited

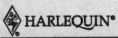

Harlequin Romance®

Coming Next Month

#3811 HIS HEIRESS WIFE Margaret Way

Olivia Linfield was the beautiful heiress; Jason Corey was the boy from the wrong side of the tracks made good. It should have been the wedding of the decade—except it never took place. Seven years later Olivia returns to Queensland to discover Jason installed as estate manager. Should she send him packing...?

The Australians

#3812 THE ENGLISHMAN'S BRIDE Sophie Weston

Sir Philip Hardesty, UN negotiator, is famed for his cool head. But for the first time in his life this never-ruffled English aristocrat is getting hot under the collar—over a woman! Kit Romaine, a girl way below his social class, is not easily impressed. If Philip wants her, he's going to have to pay!

High Society Brides

#3813 MARRIAGE IN NAME ONLY Barbara McMahon

Wealthy Connor Wolfe has no choice but to marry if he wants to keep custody of his orphaned niece. Who better as a convenient wife than his niece's guardian, Jenny Gordon? Jenny agrees—but secretly she's hoping theirs can be more than a marriage in name only....

Contract Brides

#3814 THE HONEYMOON PROPOSAL Hannah Bernard

Joanna has dreamed of marrying Matt from the day they first kissed—their wedding day, which should have been the happiest day of her life. But the relationship is a sham, and the marriage is a fake. So, if it's all pretense, why does it feel so heart-stoppingly real? And why has Matt proposed a very *real* honeymoon?